Hardbroiled

Other books by Michael Bracken

Fiction

All White Girls
Bad Girls
Canvas Bleeding
Deadly Campaign
Even Roses Bleed
In the Town of Dreams Unborn and Memories Dying
Just in Time for Love
Psi Cops
Tequila Sunrise

Other anthologies edited by Michael Bracken

Fedora: Private Eyes and Tough Guys

Hardbroiled

edited by
Michael Bracken

BETANCOURT
& COMPANY
Doylestown, Pennsylvania

Hardbroiled
A publication of
BETANCOURT & COMPANY, PUBLISHERS
P.O. Box 301
Holicong, PA 18928–0301
www.wildsidepress.com

FIRST EDITION

For Betty: Thanks for Sundays

Table of Contents

Cheating Heart

She was quick to change stories
When I showed her the shots
The room service waiter
All too glad for his part
The camera had captured
What my client had feared
His wife was caught cheating
Cheesecake and dark beer

— Stephen D. Rogers

Ramadan

Tom Sweeney

Great theater thrives in Boston. Always has.

But it's a part of my life I've tried to forget for the last twenty years, so I wasn't particularly pleased to discover Azza had accepted a job from Oscar Harrison. Azza el-Metwally is the other half — along with me, Zakaria Haddad — of A to Z Investigations. Oscar Harrison is the *bête noir* of the Boston theater scene. Half genius, half tyrant, he's the Bobby Knight of Broadway.

The job pleased me even less when I learned it involved bodyguarding. I hate bodyguarding. Like divorce work, it forces me to get entirely too personal with clients, and there's always a hidden agenda.

"Life's tough, Zakaria," Azza said, "and so is making the rent, even in East Boston. You think I like working for insurance companies between classes?"

Azza had come to the United States two years ago, in part to attend Boston University. She lived with her brother, who at the time was my partner in the East Boston PD. When Kafele — her brother — was murdered, I quit the cops and went private. Azza wanted to stay in America, and moved into an apartment over her uncle's restaurant.

Her uncle — a retired Massachusetts state cop turned cook — and his family became her new family and somehow she and I ended up as partners. She's hampered by a lack of understanding of American culture, but her work ethic is just fine.

Her eyes narrowed when I didn't answer right away. Her Egyptian heritage shows in wide, penetrating eyes and smooth, creamy-tan complexion. Her face is vaguely heart-shaped, beautiful in a classical rather than pretty way. In past millennia she would have been consort to the pharaohs.

"No," I said, after a pause. "You know I don't." Insurance work pays well, but it's the pits, especially for people like Azza and me. There are enough problems these days just being Muslim in Boston, without being hired to sneak around WASP neighborhoods, taking undercover photos of pseudo lame and halt Christians intent on ripping off Worker's Comp. "Be careful," I said. "Dump any job that doesn't feel right."

Azza dismissed this with a flip of her hand and checked her watch. "You still have time to catch Oscar this morning. He's doing pre-production for some new musical at the Center."

She smiled at me, and before I could tell her *No,* I came undone. My dead partner's youngest sister, yes, but just the sight of her curved lips and white teeth caused my pulse to climb. At forty-four, I'm exactly twice her age, but in many ways Azza is a very traditional Egyptian woman. Relative ages between men and women simply don't matter to her.

"Okay," I said. "I'll leave now. How about lunch after I talk to him?"

She frowned. "You mean dinner? Tonight?"

"I meant lunch, but dinner works fine. Has to be early, though."

Azza closed her eyes and pursed her lips. Her face hardened, becoming a cold porcelain mask. "It's Ramadan, Zakaria. We can't eat until sunset." Her mouth moved a bit, and I thought she might bring up not only my lack of fasting but also my not even being aware of Ramadan's onset. Instead, she merely said, "You certainly are Americanized, Zakaria. You cannot eat later?"

"I wish," I said. "I really do, but I have that Port Authority hearing on the new runway turn-around tonight. Probably take all night."

Azza rested her chin in her palm, elbow on the desk. "Sometimes I don't understand this country," she said. "If my family were alive, I'd return to Cairo today, and when I see what has happened to you in this country, I think maybe I should escape while I can."

Her words quenched the fire growing inside me and evidently my religious lapse dispelled her joy. She studied the ledger on her desk. "We're good at what we do, and I enjoy working with you, but we barely support ourselves. We have too many expenses — my apartment, your apartment, this office."

I backed up a step. Fresh from the Mid-East and devoutly Muslim, Azza would never hint at advancing our relationship, but such thoughts have crossed my mind. Every so often I contemplate marrying Azza. Her uncle likes me and would consent. I could provide for her, I know, but I provided for another woman, another time, in a relationship that simply couldn't have turned out worse. No need for a repeat performance. I have no reason to believe marriage to a devout Muslim would work any better than living with a non-practicing Christian woman. I shrugged into my jacket.

"Okay," I said. "I'll talk with Harrison."

I love watching actors. The drama fascinates me: the plots, the twisted love affairs both hidden and exposed, the intrigues. There isn't much actors don't do off-stage. What happens on-stage pales by comparison to actors' real lives.

A strange bunch, actors, and Boston gives them a good many theaters in which to be strange. Chief among them is the Center Theatre, a fine old proscenium theater dating back to the early twenties, tucked away down a wide alley off Tremont Street not far from the Common. Placards taped to the insides of the windows advertised an upcoming original play written, produced, and directed by the world-renowned Oscar Harrison.

Oscar might be world-renowned but he was not getting much respect today. A tall, leggy blonde stood nose-to-nose with him, and I realized they weren't practicing lines. I couldn't make out the words in Oscar's conciliatory tones, but heard the blonde repeat that she was tired of being second.

Every time Oscar stepped back, she moved up until he backed into a sofa that formed part of the set. He fell onto it with a whumph, and the blonde, sensing the dramatic moment, turned on her heel and stomped off. I gave Oscar a minute before walking through the dimmed theater to the stage.

Fiftyish, thin, and balding, his high-arched eyebrows and tight-fitting goatee made his face appear to point downward. He tended to dress more like a banker than a producer, and today wore a conservative gray suit with black wingtips. He had the conscience and morals of a banker, too. Concerning finances, his motto could easily have been: Every man for himself and the devil take the hindermost. Oscar was never hindermost.

We met on the rehearsal set. Living room furniture clumped stage right and a plywood mockup of an antique car tilted off-stage left. I rested in an easy chair; Oscar paced.

He whirled dramatically and stopped in front of me. "Are you sure you can't cover this evening?" he asked.

"Oscar, I told you. I have to testify before the City Council in East Boston, about the new turning circle for the runway nearest the marsh. Is this new star of yours in real danger? Or is this some stunt you've cooked up?"

Oscar had the grace to blush. "We do have a photo shoot tomorrow, but —" he brightened, "— Leila *has* had a sense of danger lately."

An uneasiness gurgled in my stomach, but there were probably ten thousand actresses of varying ability in Boston. Surely several were named Leila. Still . . .

Oscar spread his hands. "Sure you can't cover tonight?"

"Positive. I ran interference for the noise guy the Port Authority hired, and they want me to back up what he says. I certainly will not stand them up for whatever publicity stunt you have up your sleeve."

Oscar slumped down onto the sofa opposite me. "Why does everyone always jump to assume . . . Oh, all right, then. Meet me and Leila at the Mercy Warren House for breakfast."

I raised my eyebrows.

"Down, boy. Clare and I have a room there, also. Show up for breakfast and we'll have a war meeting. Eight o'clock?"

"In time for you to have a swarthy bodyguard on duty for the publicity stills, eh Oscar?"

He started to object but I stood and patted his arm. "Fine, Oscar. Hire someone else to baby-sit your star tonight. I'll take over tomorrow. I knew an actress named

Leila once," I added. "Good high school drama student."

"Not this one. She's the real thing, believe me. A natural. Haven't seen one this good since I pulled Clare out of one of O'Bannion's strip joints. This one will earn out the money Clare should have made for me but never did." He shook his head with a half smile. "That's what I get for marrying instead of managing her." He shook his head. "You'd think I'd learn to keep my love life separate from work, no?"

I wished I'd learned that twenty years ago. No, that's not true. I don't regret mixing love and work — I regret not being patient enough with both love and work. I might still be acting and still . . .

I clamped down on the memories and might-have-beens. "Maybe you'd better hire someone else altogether," I said.

"No, no. I want you, damn it. It's not just that Leila needs protecting — though she does, I swear — I want to put the rest of this incestuous town on notice. They've stolen my best stuff for years. With you on the job, even as a bodyguard, they'll think twice before stealing this play out from under me."

"Things that bad?" Oscar was a legend in the Beantown theater district, but come to think of it, he hadn't been in the headlines for a couple of years. Two years is forever in this what-have-you-done-lately business.

The hearing was a zoo.

I should have known better. I had thought the hardest part of my job was being an Arab and walking around Logan International Airport runways, but easily spooked airport security guards have nothing on outraged animal activists, those wealthy matrons who avert their eyes when walking by homeless beggars, but will dump time and money into saving "poor" animals.

The poor animals in this case were sea ducks. They've been known to refuse to mate when upset — don't we all — and loud noises upset them greatly.

I verified that the sound levels presented to the board were the sound levels actually measured. The guy who took the actual measurements took less heat than I did. It was his measurements that proved low flying jets didn't make enough noise to prevent sea ducks from mating, but I had nevertheless been cast as the heavy of the meeting. Maybe the Port Authority had this in mind all along: a staked goat for the animal rights people to gobble up. The upshot of six long hours of testimony was that the local animal rights groups found me guilty of *duckus interruptus* and the City Council allowed the new runway turnaround anyway.

Oscar's wife stunned me first by showing up, and then by turning out to be chief honcho of the local Protect-the-Pigeons and Save-the-Seagulls Society. Clare started the procession of interested parties who had come to testify, and her opening remarks made it clear she knew my upcoming role in the regulatory drama.

Svelte and sexy, she hung on the podium and in a breathless voice both arousing and determined, she laid out the indictment of the heartless capitalists that would despoil our planet. She acknowledged our friendship and made it clear that she valued me as a person, all the while hinting that I covered up the true sound of jet planes for the purpose of making sea ducks extinct.

After Clare came other interested but not interesting parties, then my on-deck buzzer went off and I walked backstage to wait to give my talk. They had buzzed me prematurely — I waited two and a half hours while they grilled the technician who operated the sound measuring equipment.

I presented my testimony straightforward and honestly, which didn't stop the question and answer period from turning brutal and personal. All I could do was give the facts, repeat the facts, and keep returning to the facts. This did cause a couple of my questioners to get a little testy, but I've learned not to take offense unnecessarily.

My parents moved to America when I was three years old. I grew up in New Hampshire, where almost everyone is white-skinned. Most people do not intentionally discriminate, but the pack instinct hovers just below the surface in the best of us. Fighting back, verbally or physically, invites one to be set apart from the group and therefore fair game. Keeping a low profile is the best way of defusing most situations and in truth this session could have been a lot worse. No one resorted to ethnic slurs at my repeated stonewalling.

I spent more than an hour at the podium, but eventually everyone gave up. Combined with the time I spent in the audience and in the wings waiting, I had six billable hours. That ought to placate Azza.

As soon as I left the stage Clare motioned me to the back of the hall. To my surprise, she gave me a hug.

"You did well," she said. "I'm so envious."

I held her a little longer than I would have had I not been so afraid of where Azza and I seemed to be heading. Clare and I were friends long before she auditioned for Oscar, starred in one of his Broadway revivals, and then married him. "Did well? I shot your arguments full of holes."

She waved off my comment with a delicate flip of her wrist. "This was a lost cause, but we couldn't just lie down and let them have their way without a fight, now, could we?"

I didn't see why not, tilting at windmills not being my idea of fun, but instead I said, "You knew I was to testify?"

"We take these hearings seriously, even the ones we think we can't win. Oscar knew, too. He and I fought over it last night. He didn't want me to say anything to make you look bad." She gave my arm a squeeze. "As if I could."

"What do you mean?"

Clare slipped an arm under my elbow. "I don't want to talk about Oscar. I want you to take me out to dinner."

East Boston and home are minutes away from downtown, but dinner with Clare didn't end until two in the morning. Drinks — sloe gin for her and ginger ale for me, abstinence being one of the few Muslim practices I still observe — kept us going until three o'clock. Maybe that's why I didn't notice the message light on my answering machine when I arrived home at three fifteen.

I played it back when I woke after three short hours of sleep. The message had been recorded while I waited in the wings to testify. I froze when Leila's voice spoke to me from the answering machine. It had been Leila whom Oscar hired me to protect — I should have just asked him last night. Then the tone of the message changed and I was out the door while the last word still echoed in my apartment. "Hurry."

Sluggish traffic held me back, even before seven in the morning, and I made a bad decision to take the tunnel. The Tobin Bridge might have had more traffic, but the tunnel dumped up right into the middle of the Big Dig, the largest civic highway project in history.

Once into Boston, traffic ground to an apparently permanent grid-lock around the Government Center, I parked illegally behind a construction vehicle and ran the ten blocks to the Mercy Warren House. A half dozen BPD blue-and-whites and a mile of yellow crime scene tape told me I was too late.

There were a number of ways for me to react, but mostly I didn't, falling back on old cop training to create a psychological suit of armor, focusing on facts and not letting anything get personal.

First I had to get upstairs, past the crime scene tape. In public buildings, cops often use tape merely to keep out gawkers. I strode forward, prepared to bluff my way through but Grant Dickerson, a BPD detective I'd worked with before, waved me inside. He pointed me to the seventh floor where I found Oscar, dressed in a purple bathrobe and furry brown slippers, talking to a reporter from the *Herald* while a bored cop stood nearby.

And somewhere nearby Leila lay dead.

I felt as if I was in a dream, disembodied, somehow floating in the air looking down at myself. My dream self was raging, slavering, even while in real life, my corporeal self coldly considered what to say next. My dream self finally couldn't stand it anymore and knocked the cop aside, grabbed Oscar by the throat and screamed, "Why didn't you tell me who she was? *Why?"*

Then the dream evaporated and I returned to my body. I covered the distance to Oscar in three long strides. "Who did it?" I interrupted.

Oscar flinched and twisted to face me. "That bastard O'Bannion," he said. "I've told these *officers* several times, but no one does anything." He glared at the cop, a short rumpled former prizefighter whose name I forgot. The cop rolled his eyes at me and turned away. He slipped a cigar from an inside pocket, but I knew he wouldn't light it.

I pulled Oscar into the open doorway of an adjoining room. "What makes you think O'Bannion killed her?" I asked.

"I — Are you all right, Zack?"

"Fine. What makes you think it was O'Bannion?"

"I've never seen your face so white. I —"

"Oscar, damn it, tell me about O'Bannion."

"It's not your fault, Zack. I had no idea she'd be in real danger last night. I'd have hired someone if I had thought —"

I grabbed him by his bathrobe's lapels and pulled him close. He stood frozen, eyes round and wide and mouth gaping, like a bearded fish suddenly pulled out of the water. "Tell me about O'Bannion," I said.

He nodded and I let go of his bathrobe. "You never did have any patience," he said. "Let's go to my room. We can talk privately."

I followed him down the hall. He pushed against the door leading to his suite and we walked in. My pulse hammered off the charts and I fought to get it down, but Oscar's voice was steady as he called room service for coffee and rolls. A shower splashed rhythmically behind a bathroom door that hung slightly ajar. Tendrils of steam drifted out and I pictured Janet Leigh in the shower, but Leigh's face was too blurry to distinguish. She wasn't Janet, she was . . . Who was she?

I shook my head to clear it. Oscar sat on a wide sofa covered with stiff green Victorian fabric. I sat opposite him on a stiffer-looking stuffed chair that was surprisingly comfortable. Behind Oscar ran a short hallway with the partially-closed door that led to the bathroom. An open bedroom door yielded a view of a half-made bed and a wide, mirrored dresser. A suite at the Mercy Warren House seemed expensive digs for a couple who lived only twenty-five miles away.

The chair was too comfortable. It sucked at my vitality like some sort of furniture vampire. I rubbed my forehead and pushed my back against the crinkly fabric.

"Coffee will be here soon," Oscar said, "but let's start. Bodyguarding has been overtaken by events, but I want you to prove for me that O'Bannion ruined my play."

"And killed Leila Cara."

"Yes, of course. I just said that."

"Why O'Bannion?"

"Leila was one of his girls. His latest."

"Latest what?"

"Trophy date. Whatever. She was quite a looker, you know. You ever meet her?"

"No. Never spoke with her. I followed her career for a while. UMass and the North Shore circuit."

"Well, you are the well-rounded detective, aren't you? Leila hasn't acted in two years." He shot a look at me. "She a *friend* of yours?"

"Yes. I mean, no. I never met her."

Oscar's eyebrows ramped up.

Shame flooded me. "I promised her mother I'd watch out for her." My face cooked from within, but I managed to keep my mouth shut.

Oscar waited a moment, then said, "She started going with O'Bannion two years ago. Quite a change for her, I understand, though she never did talk much about that."

"Her mother died two years ago. Cancer."

Again the eyebrows went up. This time I couldn't stop myself from saying, "Eileen Cara, her mother, and I acted together in New Hampshire for a few years. Eileen dropped out of the theater and my career fell into the crapper, so we went our separate ways." There was more to it, but I needn't share my shame with someone like Oscar.

He nodded as though all this made sense. "And you never met the girl?"

"Eileen didn't want much to do with me and we lost

contact. I saw Leila as a baby once, and then once again at her mother's funeral, but she and I didn't speak." I took a deep breath to steady myself. "Looked just like her mother, maybe even a bit prettier. Heard she was a better actress, too, but I guess I assumed she'd moved away when I didn't see her name in the theater news. You still haven't said why O'Bannion wanted to kill her."

Oscar looked at me in surprise. "Because she wouldn't go back to him. He can toss away women, but they can't leave on their own. He's a vicious bastard, you know."

"We've met."

The bathroom door opened and Clare stepped out. She wore thin cotton pajamas, wet and plastered on in those strategic places that gave away all her womanly secrets. She stumbled on the thick carpet, and her stiff-legged, over dignified recovery gave away another secret.

She did the walk that drunks walk when they don't want to look drunken. She stumbled again in front of the sofa, but managed to turn the fall into a semi-dignified plop onto the sofa next to Oscar. Each of them jerked away from the other like a pair of repelling magnets.

The three of us stared at each other until someone knocked on the door and broke the spell. A muffled voice called out, "Room Service."

Oscar brought the tray in himself and left it between Clare and me. "I recommend you both go heavy on the coffee. I shall be speaking with the police in the hallway."

Halfway to the door he turned back and said, "I'll send you a retainer later, Zack. Remember what I told you about O'Bannion. Be careful."

I expected him to slam the door, but he closed it softly. At once, Clare stood and poured a drink from a half-empty scotch bottle on a highboy by the windows. I suspect she knew how the morning sun shone through her pajamas. "Drink?" she asked.

I shook my head and she put down the glass, sloshing a little. "Neither do I," she said, but I wasn't paying attention.

Leila was dead.

I left the room with quick strides, car keys already in my hand. O'Bannion and I had done business before, and we had big business this morning.

O'Bannion lived in Marblehead, in a quaint seaside Victorian mansion built around 1850 by a whaling ship captain, but he worked in a red brick warehouse tucked in between two petroleum tank farms on a filthy canal off the Mystic River in East Boston.

A twelve-foot high chain link fence topped with razor wire surrounded his property. The wide gate to the street hung open and a couple guys stood nearby trying hard to look as if they were merely loitering. I drove past them without attracting their notice.

It was never hard to get into O'Bannion's warehouse. I'd been there before and had always gotten in easily. Getting out often became problematical, but getting out didn't matter this morning.

Inside the warehouse I let O'Bannion's bodyguards frisk me, and didn't mind when they found the holdout gun tucked into the tiny holster behind my sock. The big guy — from previous dealings with O'Bannion I knew his name to be Mike — slipped it into a pocket without comment. A professional.

The little guy looked to be the twitchy one. Lenny, I think he called himself. Wouldn't take much to send him over the edge, so I focused on him. "Ready, sweet cheeks?" I said.

Lenny's nostrils flared, but at a look from Mike he

shrugged and waved me forward. The heat of his gaze burned a spot between my shoulder blades as he followed me into O'Bannion's office, though, and I smiled to myself.

O'Bannion sat in an easy chair, a dust-jacketed novel closed in his lap. A fatuous author smiled at me from the back cover. O'Bannion stared at me silently, head slightly cocked, as though he'd just lost the conversational thread.

"You here about the girl?" he asked.

"Yeah," I said. "Harrison hired me to protect her from you. I started the job a few hours late."

O'Bannion snorted and tossed the book onto a low mahogany table. "Not me," he said.

He took the time to light a cigar and I waited until he had it going before saying, "You telling me you didn't know Ms. Cara?"

"I screwed her. Isn't that what the bible calls knowing someone?"

I started up but Mike and Lenny shifted forward. Lenny's eyes glittered. I knew I'd never reach O'Bannion, so I sat back and bided my time.

O'Bannion laid the cigar in an ashtray and stood. "Look, Zack, I don't know what you want and I don't care. Oscar Harrison made noises about me whacking this broad because I was jealous. I told the cops, and I'm telling you: she was just a broad. She's gone, now I have another one. All cats are gray in the dark, eh? If the cops need an alibi, I'll get them one. For you, I got less than nothing."

He waved an arm to Mike and we all stood. O'Bannion threw me a smirk as he walked past. He moved left to right, momentarily getting between me and Mike.

Sloppy. I sprang from the chair and unloaded a looping right that caught him under the chin. As he fell, I managed to mash his left ear with a short jab, then two hundred and fifty pounds of bodyguard landed on my back. I staggered under Mike's weight and then collapsed when Lenny's sap caught me under the right ear.

I came to slowly, sputtering, like some drunk who's had a bucket of water tossed on him. Mike stared at me as if *he'd* forgotten what we were talking about. Or maybe all the Irish mob looked that way. I looked around the room. No sign of Lenny.

I stood up. I hurt pretty bad, but not as bad as I deserved. I swung on Mike and took him by surprise. He barely managed to get an arm up in time to fend off my punch, which seemed to piss him off.

This time I stayed conscious through most of the beating.

I woke curled up into a corner of the passenger seat of my car, which was parked on one of those garbage-strewn lanes that dead end on the Chelsea River. On the other side of the oily water, in Chelsea, traffic headed into the city on the Revere Beach Parkway. The dash clock said 10:18, so I'd only been out for an hour or so. Mike sat behind the wheel, smoking.

"We was supposed to dump you in the harbor," he said. "But I talked Mr. O'Bannion out of it."

Thanks for nothing. "Why?"

"Professional courtesy."

I shifted position and felt my gun back in its clamshell holster. I stared at Mike and rubbed my legs together. My holdout gun seemed to be back in my calf holster. Mike wagged a sausage finger back and forth at me. "Uh unh," he said. "No bullets."

"Why didn't you just dump me like you were told to?" I asked.

"'Cause I know how you feel. I lost a client once. Didn't feel much like a man after. Tried to kill myself by taking on the guys who whacked my boss. Ended up killin' 'em all. Then Mr. O'Bannion hired me."

"So what?" I said.

Mike stepped out of the car and leaned back in the open window. He cocked a finger at me and let down the thumb-hammer. "Find out who killed the girl. Put that to bed, then come back to see me. If you still want to kill yourself, I'll let Lenny carve you up."

"So what?" I said again.

Mike laughed, then sighed and held up his hands in mock surrender. "Put your boy Harrison under the glass, boyo. As far as cradle-robbing bastards go, O'Bannion has nothing on him." He pivoted gracefully for so large a man and walked back toward the main street. Ten feet from the car, he turned back. "Don't forget to load your guns." He laughed again and walked away. This time he didn't turn back.

Maybe Mike had a point. Maybe not. Either way, I wasn't doing so good thrashing around, so I sat back and considered my situation.

Usually I can count on Azza to bounce things off, but I didn't want another lecture on Ramadan, about fasting during daylight hours to learn patience, inner peace, and compassion for the poor. I do okay in the compassion department, but patience and inner peace are beyond me.

How can one have inner peace with a rumbling stomach? And what's the point of fasting during daylight, anyway? What do you gain?

Thoughts raced through my brain, pulling me deeper into a black ocean of funk. Maybe I was just hungry or maybe I was about to crash and burn, I didn't know.

And the one person who could tell me I didn't want

to talk to.

Azza.

Not having her available made me realize how much I'd come to rely on her over the past two years. After Kafele was murdered, she became almost completely dependent on me. I had connections — she had nothing. Without my realizing it our positions had reversed. Although she has her own apartment, her uncle owns the building and rents only to relatives, so she has a large extended family. As her circle grew, mine shrank, and I felt as alone and helpless as I've felt.

Death would be a release, yes, and I would find it. But first I would find Leila's killer.

A measure of sanity returned and I considered. Back to basics. Who would profit from Leila's death? I knew almost nothing about her personal life, but I knew she was a star. Stars have understudies who feel they deserve top billing. A phone call to Oscar netted me a name — Mary Cummings — and an address in Somerville.

Mary lived on the fourth floor of an old dingy yellow tenement in a neighborhood comprising similarly aging, but not quite as rundown, tenements. She buzzed me in and I climbed the tilted flights of crooked and cracked stairs in a dark stairwell. The same blonde whom I had watched confront Oscar at the theater greeted me at the top, wearing an exquisite if slightly worn kimono. Her hair was pulled back in one of those rooster-comb things. It was eleven in the morning and she was fully made up.

She answered my questions willingly, but shed no light on who the possible killer might be. Her priorities differed from mine, but she had the grace to be defensive about them. "Well, of course I'm sorry she was killed," she told me. "But is my life supposed to stop?"

"You get the lead part Leila had. Is the pay much more?"

"Ri-ght." She made the word two syllables. "We get paid so much we get to live in this trash hole the theater owns. Cheaper than paying us." She lowered her voice and leaned forward as though to accentuate her next point. "What the starring role gets is exposure."

"Exposure for Broadway."

"Of course. New York people watch Boston and Philly all the time. And then there's Mr. Harrison."

"What about him?"

"Well, look what happened to Clare when she got a juicy lead part ten years ago."

"Oscar was single then."

"Oh, no, he wasn't. He was married when Clare started to work on him, but he was sure divorced by the time she finished with him. She married him and more power to her, but now they're on the outs and I'm taking my shot."

This was something I hadn't heard, either from Oscar or Clare. Clare was pushing thirty now and although she kept herself in remarkable shape, she wasn't quite the trophy wife she'd been at nineteen.

I wondered who instigated the split, and how Clare would feel if it had been Oscar who wanted out. Justice might be dispensed if she were displaced as she once displaced Oscar's previous wife, but I doubt Clare would appreciate the irony.

No need to wonder how Oscar might feel if Clare wanted out: Oscar was too wrapped up in himself to feel anything but a drive to fulfill his own needs.

And Mary? She had no idea what kind of life she faced ten years down the road. I said to her, "I hope Oscar has some money left for you after he adds Clare to the list of ex-wives he supports."

"I wouldn't worry. Even Clare couldn't spend all that insurance money."

My eyebrows shot up.

"Didn't know about that, huh? Oscar took out a million-dollar policy on Leila. Only supposed to be for a couple months, some kind of publicity thing — you know Oscar. Who knew she'd get herself killed? Some guys have all the luck."

Yeah. Some guys do. I didn't know how all this fit in, but none of the scenarios were pleasant. About the only thing I liked was that I'd concentrated so hard the last hour finding out what happened to Leila that I'd forgotten to punish myself for letting it happen.

Maybe Mike is smarter than he looks.

But then he'd almost have to be. I thanked Mary and left her to her womanly schemes. I had to talk to Oscar again.

Back at the Mercy Warren, I hurried down the hallway still chewing on Mary's last comment. The end might be in sight and I wanted to finish this. I . . . No, I stopped. I wouldn't hurry through this one. There'd be no second guessing and I had to get it right the first time.

I tried not to think about why I came to be here. Instead, I forced myself to walk slowly, to stay in the present, to focus on what was around me here and now.

There wasn't much to focus on. The hallway formed a long tunnel facing me, gold and red flocked wallpaper showing bare spots where many years worth of shoulders rubbed along it. The carpet's pattern was no longer distinguishable; the color might have once been purple or teal. The Mercy Warren House still garnered big bucks, but no longer provided big value.

Sort of like Oscar Harrison.

I had to pass the victim's room on the way to Harrison's and I averted my eyes. Before I came close to Harrison's room, Grant Dickerson popped out of an open doorway. "Haddad! Get back here!"

I debated ignoring him, but knew the futility of that from my own time as a cop.

"What do you want?" I asked.

He flashed me a look at a three-ring binder, covered in the psychedelic colors you'd expect to see on a ten-year-old girl's scrapbook. "Explain this," he said.

He stood in the doorway of Leila's room, holding out the binder. I didn't want to look at Leila's scrapbook, and I didn't want to see the place where she died. Or worse, her body if the coroner hadn't yet finished.

I wanted to remember her as I saw her last, two years ago at the funeral, so I came as close to Dickerson as I could without getting a view into the room. I stopped and held out my hand.

He waited, motionless, and for a minute we both stood there, the two feet of space between my outstretched hand and the offered binder yawning as wide as the gates of hell. I refused to meet his eyes, and after a minute he tossed the binder to me.

Taped to the cover was an eight by ten black and white photo of me, dressed in sandals and burnoose, staring defiantly at the camera. I recognized the publicity still from *Jesus Christ Superstar,* a play I did twenty years ago. My hands tingled and I almost dropped the book.

With shaking hands I opened the binder and found pictures and newspaper clippings of me, starting with *Kismet,* the play where Eileen and I met in Rochester, New Hampshire. I flipped the pages stuffed with pictures of me cut from newspapers, first in costume on different stages and then in uniform. *Globe* and *Herald* articles, pro and con, about Zakaria Haddad and Kafele el-Metwally, a pair of Egyptians partnered on the East Boston PD. An article about the east Boston PD money-laundering sting in which I played the part of a rich Saudi sheik, my most famous acting gig ever.

I saw no mention of a drunken Arab-hating redneck murdering my partner, my quitting the force and hunting down his killer, or about my taking Azza el-Metwally, my partner's sister newly arrived from Egypt, under my wing. Nothing at all about Azza and me going into business together as a private investigator team.

All these things had happened after Eileen died. This scrapbook didn't belong to Leila. It was her mother's scrapbook.

Grant led me down the hall to the elevator lobby and sat me in a chair. He reached out and took the scrapbook from my hands. "Evidence," he said with a slight apology in his voice. "You know the drill."

"Yeah," I said, "But don't lose it. I'll be putting in a claim for it."

"What's your involvement with Leila Cara?"

"Never met her."

Grant flipped through his case notebook, page by page. He took his time and didn't speak, waiting for me to break the silence. It's a old cop trick to build anxiety in a suspect, and Grant should have realized it wouldn't work on an ex-cop. He knew exactly what he intended to say, and he and I both knew it. Still, he paused, pretended to read, and frowned. "You met her twice, I've been told."

"Who told you that?"

"You admit it, then?"

"Look, Grant, let's stop being cute here and put all our cards on the table, okay?" I paused, wondering how few cards I had to show him to make him go away and leave me alone.

"I knew the victim's mother a long time ago," I said, "We both acted in New Hampshire. Then our acting careers nose-dived and we split. She found a job in New Hampshire; I became a cop in East Boston. I was in the big sheik sting in '91, then you Boston guys borrowed me a few times for your own stings, and then I figured I could make more money going private."

"Is this going anywhere, Haddad?"

"Bear with me. The victim's mother and I lost contact. The next time I saw her she had a baby — Leila — but no husband. The only other time I was in the same room as the victim was at her mother's funeral two years ago. The victim and I didn't speak. I haven't seen or heard of her since."

Grant made a few scratches in his notebook, then looked up, waiting for me to continue. "And," he said.

"That's it. What else can I tell you?"

"You could tell me how you happened to be here."

"Oscar Harrison hired me to guard her. I was to start this morning. Oscar only called the woman Leila; I had no idea she was Eileen's daughter until she . . . until this morning."

Grant looked up, but didn't pursue the hitch in my voice. "Oscar will verify this, of course," he said.

"If he hasn't already. Check with Azza. She took his call, not me."

Grant wrote a couple more minutes, occasionally squinting as he wrote. "You know more about this than you're saying, Haddad."

"If I told you everything I knew, I'd be out of a job."

"Maybe, but this is more than a job. This is personal for you."

"Taken up mind reading, have you?"

Grant shook his head, slowly and without emotion, but resolutely. "Something's off here. What happened to your face?"

"Run in with two of O'Bannion's boys."

"Oscar says O'Bannion did the girl."

"I don't think so," I said.

"Neither do I. The girl's head was smashed with a prop

from the play. O'Bannion wouldn't get cute like that. He'd just pop her. Or have his boys do it."

"For once I agree with you. Can I go talk to Oscar now?"

"Why'd you go brace O'Bannion if this isn't personal?"

I'd held it in all morning, but his pushing snapped my patience. I jumped out of the chair, arms wide. "It *is* personal, you stupid bastard! Someone murdered the girl I was supposed to protect. You think this is just business?"

Grant pushed me back against the wall. "Get smart with me and you'll be sitting in a cell downtown. You're covering something."

I shoved his arm away, still pissed and irrational. "Think I killed her, do you?" My breath caught in my chest. In a way I had killed her. Inaction allowed becomes an action.

"You'll know when I think you had a part in this because you'll be in cuffs before you can blink. Now, where were you last night?"

"You already know my whereabouts last night. Clare and I were both at a city council meeting from six o'clock to past midnight, then we had dinner. I left her at three in the morning. When did you say Leila died?"

"Around ten. Cozy for you two to alibi each other."

"I have work to do. Book me or release me."

Grant stepped aside, but grabbed my arm as I passed by. "Don't count on friendship, Haddad. Friendship don't mean squat in this business."

So I'm finding out.

"In this business, there are no friends, only clients."

Dickerson turned and walked back into the murder room. I tried the door of Oscar's room, but it was locked and he didn't answer my pounding. I retreated to the elevator lobby and held my thumb against the DOWN button until the elevator arrived.

Oscar wasn't at the Mercy Warren and he wasn't at the Center Theatre. One of the tech crew, a skinny white kid with dirty blond dreadlocks, told me he was probably at the Yellow House.

The Yellow House, he explained with a leer, was where the theater put up their players. Oscar was probably doing some couch auditioning, he said.

Then I put together what the kid just told me and what Grant had said to me about alibis and it all fell into place. I pulled out my cell phone and called Clare's room, but no one answered. I called the cops, then bolted to my car to race them to the Yellow House.

A Lexus with the license plate THEATR was parked on the street. No blue and whites were in sight, but I couldn't wait for them. I kicked in the door and ran for the stairs. On the second landing I heard a pair of muffled shots above and sirens outside. Hoping the cops had a couple young sprinters who would get up here in a hurry, I took the steps two at a time to the fourth floor and flung open the landing door.

Mary lay on the floor, bleeding on the faded carpet. The door to her room hung open.

The left shoulder of her kimono was blood-sodden and bright red blood spurted from an ugly hole in her thigh.

I stripped off my belt and quickly tied a tourniquet around the bleeding leg. When I yanked it tight, her eyes jerked open. She tried to say something, but only a bit of spittle escaped her mouth.

Some sixth sense warned me. I popped my gun from its holster and spun around to see Clare step into the room and point a pistol at me.

She fired and I fired back reflexively. Her shot thudded into the floor; mine slammed squarely in her chest.

She flew backwards and I managed not to pull the trigger again. Damn it! I shouldn't have shot. She had pointed the gun away from me on purpose.

I holstered my pistol and ran to her. She was still alive, but not for long — my bullet had left a fist-sized exit wound below her right shoulder blade. There was no way I could stop the flow of blood, but I took off my coat and crammed it against the hole.

"I didn't mean to shoot at you," she gasped. "I thought for a second you were Oscar."

"I know," I said.

She spat out a little blood. "I pulled the gun to the side just as I fired."

"I know. I didn't realize in time and shot back."

"He wanted to leave me. I thought he'd been fooling around with Leila, but it was Mary all along. I came here hoping to catch her and Oscar together. She was alone and I shot her. Then when you came in I thought you were him." A coughing jag seized her and she stiffened.

"Don't talk now," I said. "Help will be here in a minute."

But ten seconds later when the cops burst through the stairway door, she was dead.

Rural Cemetery was once out in the country, but even New Hampshire towns expand given time. The city of Rochester has grown since Eileen and I acted in a different musical every week at the old Rochester Music Theater. The city had already grown close to the cemetery when Eileen had been buried two years ago, and since then housing developments had completely surrounded it.

I sat on the grass before Eileen's plain grave marker, a pair of roses in hand, not knowing what to say.

I listened to the sound of the wind in the pines for a few minutes, and the occasional truck out on the Spaulding Turnpike. A bee hummed its way through an errant patch of clover behind a nearby grave marker, and I studied its flight, trying to discover its pattern of movement, until it flew off.

Then I could delay no longer and I faced her gravestone squarely. "I never listened to you much when we lived together, Eileen. Maybe that's why I did what you said and stayed away from Leila. I told you I'd watch out for her, but God forgive me, I couldn't do it. I couldn't stand seeing my daughter and not being able to approach her, to talk to her, to hold her. Except for your funeral, I haven't seen her in years. I didn't even know she was in Boston. Maybe if I had . . .

"I'm sorry, Eileen. You live with your God now, and you probably know as well as I do what is happening. You may even feel worse than I do, if that's possible. I just want you to know her death is my fault, not yours. You asked me to stay away, to let her be, but I didn't have to do what you asked. I wish to God I hadn't."

I waited for a sign, but heard only the wind. "But I did obey you and I did avoid her and now she's dead and it's my fault and I never spent even a single day with my daughter. I never once held her hand." The last words choked me on the way out, and I fell over onto my side, gasping for breath.

When my chest stopped heaving, I wiped my eyes and placed a rose on Eileen's headstone. The roses had come with cards. This one I had signed Zakaria. At my request Eileen had always called me Zack, my poor attempt to fit into her culture. Only when we made love did she forget and call out an impassioned *Zakaria* and now I wished I could hear her say my name again.

I stood up when I was able. I had more to say, but I

never did know how to tell Eileen how I felt. Maybe if I had, she and I would have married and Leila would be alive today.

I had one more rose to deliver. This card I had signed Zakaria abu Leila: Zakaria, father of Leila.

I had given up more than my religion twenty-five years ago, when I couldn't wait to become an *American.* I had given up my heritage, also. A parent's pride is perhaps an Egyptian's greatest joy, and I had abandoned it as well as my daughter, all because of what now seemed petty differences between Eileen and me, and because I didn't have the patience to resolve them.

The realization staggered me.

Lack of patience was more than a personal quirk of mine. It was the defect of my life, the black blot on my soul. Lack of patience worked to destroy me and everyone around me.

The lack of patience in allowing time for our different cultures to combine had caused me to give up Eileen, and so my daughter. Lack of patience, the need for immediate absolution, caused me to try to kill myself using O'Bannion's bodyguards.

Patience I would have learned had I only practiced my faith. I closed my eyes, but couldn't stop thinking. Patience isn't learned, I suddenly realized. It is practiced. Through Ramadan, daily fasting requires daily patience. One accepts that food will come in its time, as all things come in their own time. Had I only kept my faith, had I only observed the fasting of Ramadan, had I only . . . had I only . . . had I only . . .

Oh, Leila, Eileen, I'm so sorry.

Leaving the rose on Eileen's headstone was one of the hardest things I've ever done in my life. I walked back to my car weary with the knowledge that delivering the second rose would be infinitely harder.

But also I knew this: I would honor Ramadan. I would call Azza and apologize, and ask her to have dinner with me after sunset.

Atonement will come when Allah wills it, and I will wait for that time.

One Lousy Piece of Toast

Dan Sontup

The three of us sat quietly in the booth, not talking for the moment, frosted beer mugs in front of us waiting to be lifted. It was dim and cool inside the bar, and the summer afternoon traffic on the Vermont highway outside was just a sort of pleasant hum in the background.

"Good to see you again, Hank," Al said after a while.

My uncle Henry nodded, picked up his beer and looked at it, then took a swallow. "Sorry I didn't ask you out to the house, Al."

"It's okay. Easier for us to talk out here, anyhow." He turned to me, quickly changing the subject. Howya been doin', Ed?"

"Good." I lifted my mug and put it to my lips.

"Up here for a weekend visit, you said?"

I nodded and took a quick swallow.

"Business okay?"

I shrugged. "Hustling right along, Al. But I'm not complaining."

Al chuckled. "Anything exciting happening down

there in Boston, Mr. Private Eye?"

I gave him a small smile, sensing what he was trying to do about Uncle Henry's obvious mood, and going along with it.

"We like to call ourselves private investigators, Al," I said. "And no, nothing real exciting. Just the usual divorce work, skip tracing, and industrial security." I grinned at him. "Nothing like all that real excitement you must roll around in there in Frisco, right?"

"We like to call it San Francisco out there, sonny." He grinned right back at me.

"Listen to him, Uncle Henry," I said. "Not even two years away from here and already he thinks he's a native-born Californian."

It didn't work. All the kidding around that Al and I had done to perk up Uncle Henry didn't have any effect on him. He raised his beer and took a long swallow and set the mug down heavily on the table. "I should've asked you out to the house regardless," he said.

Al looked away for a moment. "How's Millie these days?"

"The same."

"Her heart any better?"

Uncle Henry shook his head. "Not any worse either," he said after a moment.

"What does the doc say?"

"Just what he always says. If Millie takes it real easy and watches herself carefully, there's no reason she can't live years more."

"But Aunt Mille doesn't ever take anything easy," I said. "She's never learned to relax."

Uncle Henry gave me a bleak stare.

Al drained his mug and wiped froth from his bushy white mustache. "Another?"

I looked down at my half-full mug and shook my head.

Uncle Henry lifted his mug and tilted his head back and gulped it down. "Yeah."

Al motioned to the bartender. Two frosty mugs of cold beer were placed in front of us.

"You're looking good," Al said to my uncle.

"Quit lying."

Al grinned. "Well, you're not looking all that bad, Hank. Let's see, when was I up here last? About a year ago, right?"

"That's right," I said. "It was in the summer."

"Well," Al said to my uncle, "I gotta say you don't look any worse now then you did then, old buddy."

"It's not how I look. It's how I feel inside."

Al and I said nothing.

"Dead," my uncle said.

"Come on now, Hank," Al said, giving me a sidelong questioning glance.

"Dead. That's just how I feel."

"For a man in his sixties and in good health, you talk like a damn fool," Al said, and I could see he was trying to keep his tone light and easy.

"Dead, I tell you. I'm dead inside."

Al looked down at the table and turned the beer mug in his hands. "Maybe all you need is a change of scenery," he said quietly, and I knew right away where this was leading, but there was no way to stop it.

Uncle Henry looked away.

"Can't you manage even a little trip?" Al said. "Maybe come out and visit with me. I'm leaving tomorrow, but —"

"Forget it, Al."

"Well, look, I didn't mean you should come out with me right now. Maybe a little later. You can come anytime you're ready. Ed here can drive you down to Burlington, and all you gotta do is hop on a jet, and you'll be out there with me in just a few hours. We'll have ourselves a high old time. I'm telling you, Hank, it's —"

"I said forget it, Al."

"Why?"

"Millie."

"Oh."

"I can't leave her. Got to look after her."

"But she's not bedridden."

"Might as well be."

Al gave me another sidelong look. "Maybe Ed can look after her for a few days."

My uncle and I quickly shook our heads.

"She's got no use for me," I said.

"That's the truth," my uncle Henry said. "She hasn't liked him since he was a kid." He grunted. "She hasn't really liked anybody most of her life, for that matter."

Al looked at him thoughtfully. "You think maybe — just maybe — she might want to make the trip out there with you? Sort of a vacation, you know."

Uncle Henry snorted.

"I'm sorry, Hank," Al said. "It was just a thought."

Uncle Henry took a long swallow of his beer.

Al cleared his throat. "I — I was hoping things might be a little different for you by now, Hank. That's one of the reasons I came back this time."

Uncle Henry looked at him. "The shop?"

Al nodded. "I'm just about ready to close the deal. In another six months at most, the owner will be ready to sell. I can't swing it all by myself. I need a partner like I told you the last time. Not only for the finances, but someone who has the skills for repairing small appliances. Hank, you're the only one I know who fills the bill — and you're my best and oldest friend, to boot."

Uncle Henry looked down at the table.

"Damn!" Al said softly.

Uncle Henry took a swallow of his beer.

"It wouldn't take much money," Al said. "It's a real small shop."

"I got eight hundred in the bank," Uncle Henry said. "And you know how much I make out at the factory." He shrugged. "Which ain't likely to last much longer. They're talking closing down."

Al shook his head slowly.

Uncle Henry stared down at the beer mug in his hands and said, "I got no way to raise the money even if I was free to go. I got group and health insurance out at the plant, but there's no cash value on it. I got no other insurance or stocks or a 401k or a pension or anything like that. The only thing is the house. That's bought and paid for, but the way things are going now, we may have to refinance if I lose my job." He raised the mug to his lips and said, "Better look for another partner, Al," and took a big gulp, tilting his head back.

Al sighed. "I was sort of hoping you — or maybe even you and Millie — could come down and look things over. The shop is in a suburb of Los Angeles. It's a beautiful location." He sighed again, heavier this time. "I can't do it without you, Hank. I don't want to do it without you, and that's a fact. You're my old friend."

"That won't change," Uncle Henry said.

Al nodded, and a distant look came into his eyes. "It's a damn shame, that's what it is. You're just about the best small appliance repairman I know. You got a way with tools and with fixing things that nobody else I know can match. I'm good at electronics, but the whole world isn't all electronic, you know. There are still plenty of toasters and food mixers and vacuum cleaners out there that break down and need someone to get them working again. Hell, with my business hustle and your talent for repairing things we could really make that shop hum. Think of it, Hank. No more cold winters up here for you and Millie, sunshine and green things growing all year round, the two of us working together, and on weekends —"

"Shut up, Al. Please just shut up."

Al took a long swallow of his beer. "Sorry, Hank. This has been a dream of mine for a long time now. I'm . . . well, I tell you, Hank, in a word, I'm desperate."

Uncle Henry and I glanced at him.

"Yeah . . . desperate," Al said. "I can feel everything slipping away from me, Hank. There's no future."

"Don't talk like that, Al," I said.

He looked at me, and I could see something deep in his eyes, a sadness that had never before surfaced in the Al I knew from childhood.

He turned to my uncle Henry. "I need you, old friend. I really need you." His eyes clouded. "We're all that's left of the old gang. I never married, got no family. Got no real friends except you . . ." His voice trailed off.

The opening of the outer door brought a sudden rush of traffic noise from outside, and the frame of a large fat man filled the doorway.

"Hey, isn't that Chief Benson?" Al whispered.

"Yeah, that's him," I said.

The three of us watched as the chief made his way across the room. He hadn't seen us yet.

"Old bastard hasn't really changed," I said, looking at the enormous bulk of the man in his blue short-sleeved uniform shirt, badge over the left pocket, gun belt on his ample hip weighted down with a holstered .38 revolver and handcuffs and a row of deadly-looking cartridges lining the belt.

He suddenly spotted us, and his fleshy face cracked open in a broad, knowing grin that was more like a leer. He came over to the booth, moving his huge body with some effort.

"Well, well," he boomed out as he flicked his gaze over

us. “Look who’s here. How you been, Al?”

“I’m doing okay, Chief.”

“Visiting the old home town?”

“Going back tomorrow.”

“Sunny California, eh?”

“That’s right. Can’t take these cold Vermont winters anymore.”

Chief Benson grunted and swiveled his big head and stared at me with hard eyes behind puffy eyelids. “See you’re here too, Ed.”

I didn’t answer him.

“Staying out of trouble down there in Boston?”

He spat out the word *trouble,* and I was suddenly back again as a teenager being harassed almost every weekend by Benson — all of which started when he found a bunch of us smoking weed behind the high school. We scattered, and he took off after me, maybe because I stopped for a quick last puff before I threw away the stub, and by then I was the only one left of the group. It was too dark there for him to recognize me, and I made sure to keep my back to him as I ran. He was a patrol cop then and almost as fat as he was now, and I ran easily away from him, hearing him panting and breathing hoarsely as he tried to get to me. I ducked into some woods and let out a loud laugh, taunting him. He came crashing through the underbrush, and I took off again.

I made it to Al’s house and knocked at the back door, and Al let me in with a questioning look on his face. I told him the situation in a couple of quick sentences while we heard Benson lumbering into the back yard. Al grinned and motioned for me to follow him. We went into the living room where Al had the TV going, and I flopped down on the couch and took a deep breath.

Benson banged on the back door. Al went and let him in. Benson came into the living room and glared at me. I looked up at him with what I hoped was innocence written all over my face.

It was over with quickly. Al told Benson I had been with him watching TV for the last couple of hours. Benson bellowed and accused Al of covering up for me and lying so I'd have an alibi, but there was nothing Benson could do about it. He left, but the hard, unblinking look he gave me was chilling, and I watched my step around him from then on.

From the way he was looking at us now in the bar, it was clear he still remembered and had added chunks of hate with each pound he had put on his body since that night.

"Plenty of trouble in Boston, Chief," I said evenly, "but nothing I can't handle."

"Big shot private eye, so I hear."

I shrugged.

"They let you carry a piece?"

"Got a license, but I don't often carry."

"You carrying now?"

"No."

Benson grunted. "Don't let me find out different. You got no license up here in this state."

I didn't answer him, but he wouldn't let it go.

"You think you can handle trouble down there in Boston," he growled at me, "but it'd be a lot different kind of trouble you'll get from me you step out of line even a little bit."

I stared at him silently, then deliberately broke eye contact, like I was too bored with the conversation to keep on with it.

Benson turned to my uncle Henry. "How're you doing, Hank?"

"I'm okay, Chief."

"And Millie?"

"Same as always."

"Tell her I said hello."

Uncle Henry nodded. Benson gave Al a long look, then did the same to me, and turned and walked away. We watched him head over to the bar and slap his big fist on the worn wood and bellow at the bartender, "I got a tip you been serving minors in here. You and me got some talking to do."

Al and I looked at each other. Uncle Henry finished his beer and set the mug down. "Well," he said, "that did sort of spoil the moment."

Al stood and moved out of the booth. "Time to go anyhow."

We left the bar and I gave Al a lift back to his motel, where Uncle Henry and I had picked him up earlier.

"I don't have to leave till late in the day tomorrow," Al said, getting out of the car. "Maybe we can get together again someplace where Chief Benson isn't likely to show up."

Uncle Henry nodded, and I said, "Sounds good to me."

Al gave us a brief wave and turned and walked back to his room. Uncle Henry sighed. "Might as well head for home." He gave me a quick look. "You're coming in with me, right?"

"Well, I don't know . . ."

"I want you to, Ed." He stared through the windshield. "I tell you the truth, I can't face Millie alone just now. Stay a couple hours, Ed. It'll help me."

"Sure, Uncle Henry." I started the car and pulled out of the motel parking lot.

Twenty minutes later, when we walked into the house, I began to regret telling him I'd stay. We'd hardly closed the door behind us when Aunt Millie's voice screeched out from the living room, "Where the hell have you been?"

Uncle Henry cringed into his shoulders and turned so I couldn't see his face. I knew I was asking for it, but I called out, "He was with me, Aunt Millie. We stopped for a beer."

There was a long moment of silence, then she shouted, "And just who the hell are you?"

I sighed and looked at Uncle Henry. He wouldn't meet my gaze. I walked into the living room. "It's me, Aunt Millie — Ed."

She damn well knew my voice, and I could see the gleam of satisfaction in her eyes as she turned to me and looked me up and down, getting her jollies, as always, by yanking my chain. She was sitting in the old recliner that I knew Uncle Henry used to claim as his own, but which she had now clearly appropriated for herself. She had the footrest up and was leaning back, her blue-flowered housedress straining at the seams as she adjusted her position. She ran Chief Benson a close second in the body-bulk department, only hers was more a sloppy, jellylike quivering fat.

"Went out for a beer, is that what you're telling me?" she said to me, her voice just a bit lower than the screech that had greeted us when we first came in.

"Yes, we did, Aunt Millie."

Uncle Henry came into the room behind me at that moment. She glared at him. "You'd better be sober. I need some help here." She waved at the TV set where a talk-show host was smiling and thanking each one of his guests as the audience applauded and whistled their appreciation. "Switch it to Channel 2," she commanded.

Uncle Henry gave a quick glance at the remote in her hand, then walked to the TV set and switched channels.

"And you might as well throw out this remote." She thrust it at him. "I told you before it was going bad, and now the damn thing is broke."

He took the remote from her and studied it.

"What're you looking at it for? You already told me you can't fix it."

"It's all electronics inside, Millie."

"Yeah, I know. You're the great Mr. Fix-It, right? Don't make me laugh."

"I don't know electronics that good, Millie. You already know that."

"All I know is you're standing in front of the TV. I can't see through you, dummy."

Uncle Henry moved to one side. A commercial was on the screen now, and she glanced up at him as he stood there looking down at the remote in his hand. "And another thing," she said, her voice rising again to near-screech level. "That lousy toaster isn't working."

"What's wrong with it?"

"It just stops, and those little wire things inside don't get red anymore. I have to shake it and yank the cord around to get it started again."

"Probably needs a new cord," I said to Uncle Henry, hoping that by butting in I might take her focus away from him for at least a moment.

He looked at me and nodded. "Could be. I got a spare cord in the garage."

"Well, don't just stand there," Aunt Millie shouted at him. "Go get it and fix the damn toaster. You should know by now that I like my toast done just right, and the least you could do is make sure I get it. You do little enough around here as it is."

I looked at Aunt Millie and remembered what had always been her love affair with toast. It was more than the texture and color of the bread had to be just right when it popped up in the toaster. To her, it meant a thick piece of toast slathered with lots of butter and marmalade — a pleasure that she indulged in several times a day, never mind just at breakfast. I was sure the doctor had told her this wasn't doing her heart any good, but then Aunt Millie probably thought little better of the doctor than she did of Al and me.

"Uh, Millie . . . ," Uncle Henry said.

"What now?"

"About the remote."

She stared at him. "What about it? You can't fix it, you get me a new one. Is that simple enough for you to understand?"

"Well, I saw Al today, and —"

"I had a hunch that was where you were sneaking off to. You didn't fool me one bit. Al's an old bum. You should know better than to even mention his name to me."

"It's just that Al knows more about remotes than I do, Millie. He can pick up a good replacement while I'm fixing the toaster."

"And bring it here? And come into my house? You listen to me, old man —"

"You need a remote right now," Uncle Henry said quickly, cutting her off before she could get any more steamed up. "This is the night where you watch a lot of programs, you know, and —"

She waved her hand, silencing him. The commercial was about to end. "Okay, okay. Do it that way. Just make sure you keep the old bum away from me and get him out of here fast."

"I'll take care of it," Uncle Henry said. "I'll take care of everything."

She grunted at him, her eyes fastened to the TV as the program started, this one a courtroom setting with a snippy, sarcastic female judge on the bench.

Uncle Henry looked at her for a long moment, then at me, then walked quickly out of the room. I heard the back door in the kitchen open and close even before I could get out of the living room. I went into the kitchen and out the door and over to the garage. Uncle Henry was in there, rummaging around in a box under his workbench. He straightened up with an electric cord in his hand.

We went back into the kitchen silently. He took the toaster from the shelf over the sink and brought it over to the kitchen table.

"I think I'll take off now, Uncle Henry," I said.

He nodded. "Thanks for sticking around, Ed."

"Maybe tomorrow we'll get together again with Al before the two of us leave," I said.

"Maybe."

I didn't know what else to say. I went to the back door and paused with my hand on the knob and looked back at him. He was staring in the direction of the living room where Aunt Millie slouched and spread in the recliner and from where the shrill voice of the TV judge was laying down the law to the people in front of her in her court. And my Uncle Henry now had the electric cord in both hands, clenching it in his fists, stretching it taut, while he stood motionless and stared at the archway entrance to the living room.

I opened the door silently and left.

We didn't get together the next day, as we had planned. Uncle Henry was stuck in the house taking care of some chores Millie insisted he get done, and Al arranged to take an earlier flight. But three weeks later, the three of us were back again in the same booth in the bar, beer mugs once again on the table in front of us.

"It was good of you to come," Uncle Henry said.

"That's what old friends are for," Al said.

"I mean," Uncle Henry said, "Ed here is family and

lives pretty close in Boston, but it's less than a month since you were here last, and I know it costs money to fly back and forth from the coast like that. I want you to know that I really appreciate this, Al."

"Like I said, Hank, what else are friends for if you can't count on them when you need them."

Uncle Henry nodded slowly.

"Well," Al said, looking at me for a moment and then back to Uncle Henry, "I guess the old house is going to seem a bit empty now."

Uncle Henry nodded again.

"She had a good funeral," I said.

"She always liked autumn days like this, didn't she, Hank?" Al said.

"Yes, she did . . . a long time ago."

"I — I think I'll miss her," I said. "I mean . . ."

Uncle Henry looked at me with a sad smile. "I know what you mean, Ed." He took a deep breath. "You'll miss the old Aunt Millie . . . and I'll miss the Millie I once loved and married." He took another breath. "But that Millie left me a long time ago. This — this one — wasn't the same person. I won't miss her. That's the honest truth, and I'd be a damn liar if I said otherwise."

We were silent for a while, staring down into our beer mugs. Then Al said, "Look, Hank, we haven't had a chance to talk much since I got here, and this may be the wrong time for it, but —"

The door flew open, and the bulk of Chief Benson charged in. He came right over to our booth and stood there looking down at us, his eyes even deeper in his fleshy face than I had ever seen, with little pinpoints of light flickering in the dark of his eyes as he swept his gaze from one of us to the other.

"Thought I'd find the three of you here," he said, his voice rasping out. He turned to Uncle Henry. "I've already expressed my condolences to you at the funeral, Hank, so I won't repeat them now, especially with what I got to tell you this time."

Uncle Henry looked up at him, his face calm.

"You know I took that toaster," Benson said.

Uncle Henry nodded.

"Sent it to the state lab," Benson said.

Al started to speak, then clamped his mouth shut. I kept my eyes on Chief Benson's face.

"It was involved in her death," Benson said. "I wanted it checked out. It was evidence."

"Evidence of what, Chief?" I said.

He didn't even look at me. He stared straight at Henry and said, "You told us she poked at a live shorted-out toaster and the shock was what killed her, electrocuted her and stopped her weakened heart like the doc said."

"That's right," Uncle Henry said. "I'd told her over and over again not to use a knife to poke at the toaster when a piece of bread got stuck. Told her to unplug the toaster first." He started to pick up his beer mug, then put it down. "She didn't pay any attention to what I said . . . she never did."

"You had just repaired that toaster, right?" Benson said.

"Wouldn't call it a repair job. Just needed a new cord, that's all."

The chief raised a meaty right hand and jabbed in the air at Uncle Henry with his extended thick forefinger. His voice dropped to a low menacing tone. "Then why did you field strip that toaster all the way down? The boys at the lab tell me it was clear that the toaster had been disassembled and put back together again very recently. They also told me that it's a simple matter to replace a cord. Just remove a cover on the bottom of the toaster and take out the old cord and connect a new one. No need at all to disassemble the whole toaster."

"That's true," Uncle Henry said, his face still calm, his voice steady. "And, yes, I did take the toaster apart."

"Why?" The chief's voice was even lower and more menacing.

Uncle Henry gave a brief shrug. "The old cord seemed to be working all right. I yanked on it and pulled it, and the toaster still operated okay. So, I thought it might be something else and took the toaster apart." He paused for a moment. "It wasn't something else. It turned out it was the cord after all."

Chief Benson grunted, and a sly look spread over his face. "Tell me, Hank, when you had that toaster all apart in front of you, did you happen to look at and maybe pick up the —" He frowned and reached into his shirt pocket and took out a small memo book and flipped the pages. "— the thermostatic element?"

"If I had the toaster stripped down, I guess I would've had to handle the thermostat. Sure. Why do you ask, Chief?"

"Because the lab boys tell me that a metal strip in the thermostat had come loose or —" The sly look was even more pronounced now. "— or maybe had been deliberately loosened. You know what that means, Hank? I'll tell you. It means that when Millie poked enough times at a piece of sticking toast — as you knew damn well she would — the metal strip eventually worked all the way loose and shorted out the toaster, and that — that was what delivered the fatal shock to her. That was what killed her."

Uncle Henry looked thoughtful, then picked up his beer and took a long swallow. "I didn't look close at the thermostatic control. Just put it to one side along with all the other parts. If I had looked more closely, I might have found the loose metal strip. That's a fact. And it's also a fact that maybe that's what caused the short that killed

Mille." He picked up his beer mug, then set it down again without drinking. "I do blame myself for that, Chief."

"Not your fault, Uncle Henry," I said quickly. "Not your fault at all. You had no way of knowing."

"Shut up," Benson said without even looking at me.

"What's your point, Chief," Uncle Henry said, "outside of trying to lay a guilt trip on me?"

"My point, Hank, in case you've forgotten, is that the lab boys tell me the metal strip could have been deliberately loosened."

"And you think I did that?"

"You're damn right I do."

"Then that would mean I set out to murder Millie."

"Bingo," the chief said.

"So are you here to arrest me?"

Benson glared at him. "In time, in due time, Hank."

"You mean you don't have any real evidence, isn't that it, Chief?" I said. "You're just fishing."

"Shut up," Benson said again, still without looking at me, letting me know that I wasn't worth the bother of glaring at me. "I'm not fishing, Hank. I know just what I'm doing." He hitched up his gun belt over his huge stomach. "Let me tell you what I've got so far." He began to tick off points on his sausage fingers. "First, motive. It's been no secret around town that your good old buddy, Al here, has been trying to talk you into coming out to California and opening a shop with him. He's talked about it enough each time he comes out here, so lots of people know this. And lots of people also know that Millie's been sick for a while now, and the doc didn't violate any patient privilege when he told me about her weak heart. It all came out at the inquest, anyhow. And next, a little check of the records at town hall show me that you own your house free and clear, and it's all yours now that Millie's dead. So maybe you got tired of waiting for her to pass on and give you the chance to hook up with your buddy Al. And so when you laid the fatal trap for Mille and finished working on the toaster and put it together again and —"

"No, he didn't, Chief," Al said.

Benson swiveled his bull neck and stared at Al.

"He didn't put the toaster together again," Al said before the chief could speak. "I did."

"You what?"

"I said I was the one who put the toaster together, Chief."

"And you're just telling me that now?"

"It didn't come up until now."

"You're telling me that Hank took the toaster apart and that you put it together again for him?"

"That's right, Chief." Al said.

"I want the truth. I want all of it now."

"I picked up a new TV remote for Hank," Al said, "so Millie would be able to watch her programs without bother. I took a taxi, and when I got there, Millie shouted for me to stay in the kitchen and that Hank should bring her the remote — and then she wanted me out of the house. Hank took it in to Millie, and I heard him trying to explain to her how to use it. I saw the stripped-down toaster on the kitchen table. Hank had told me before he went in to Millie that he had checked out the toaster and all it needed was to replace the cord with the one he had left on the table. I thought I'd give him a hand, so I started putting everything together. Millie kept Hank with her a long time while she yelled at him and said he was too stupid to know anything about the remote, and when he said he'd bring me in to explain it to her, she screamed at him and told him he was a dummy and it went on and on like that until finally Hank got it all straightened out for her and he came back to the kitchen."

"And that's it?" Benson growled. "That's all of it?"

"Well, by the time Hank came back, I had the toaster just about all reassembled, and I hooked up the cord and finished the job while Hank sat at the kitchen table with his head in his hands. I told him to hang in there, and then I called for a taxi and went back to my motel." He waited a moment, then added, "I didn't look closely at the thermostat, either."

Benson frowned, his forehead wrinkling with the effort. "So, what we have now is either one of the two of you could have monkeyed with that thermostat, right?"

"If that's what you want to think, Chief," Al said.

"The two of you each handled all the toaster parts."

"That's about the size of it, Chief."

Benson's face reddened. "Still up to your old tricks, huh, Al? Still covering up and giving alibis." He turned and finally looked at me, and the hate in his eyes told me that he was remembering the incident in back of the high school. I didn't let him stare me down.

Benson swung back to Al and Uncle Henry and said, "I'm looking at a murderer here. Maybe one, maybe two working together."

"That'll be just about enough of that!" Uncle Henry said, his voice rising.

"You telling me what I can or can't say, Hank?"

"I'm telling you it was an accident, just like it was ruled at the inquest. If you're not going to make an arrest here, I think you'd better just leave us alone."

I could see Benson's big fists clench. His right hand moved slightly toward his holstered gun. I tensed in the booth, ready to move fast if I had to.

Benson suddenly relaxed. He looked at each one of us in turn, then swung around and headed for the door. With his hand on the doorknob, he turned back to us and said, "I'm not done with you, yet. Count on it." He opened the door and slammed it behind him as he left.

We looked at each other, then Uncle Henry said, “I’ve made up my mind, Al. I’m coming out to California with you. I’ll be out there as soon as I can settle things about the house here.”

And that was it. We didn’t talk much after that. There was nothing much that could be said. I dropped Uncle Henry off at his house and took Al back to his motel where he picked his luggage, and then we headed for the highway to the airport.

We were silent for most of the ride, and then, when we were close to exit for the airport, Al said, “Chief Benson is dumb as a block of granite.”

“I wouldn’t be too sure of that,” I said.

Al glanced at me. “You think he’s got it all figured out?”

“I didn’t say that, Al.”

“You think I did it, don’t you.”

I kept my eyes on the road. “Why should I think that?”

“I’m a desperate man, remember? I said that the last time.”

“Uncle Henry is a desperate man, too.”

“So, you think maybe Chief Benson was right and that Hank set things up so Millie would kill herself?”

“I didn’t say that, either.”

“Then just what are you saying, Ed?”

“Well, for one thing, you didn’t do it, Al.”

“Oh, you know that, do you?”

“It’s a logical deduction.”

“Arrived at through that keen detective mind of yours, right?”

“Maybe.”

“And why are you so sure I didn’t do it, Ed?”

“You know electronics, Al. You don’t know all that much about toasters and thermostatic controls.”

“I was fixing toasters before you were born, sonny.”

"And another thing, you wouldn't take a chance on Hank touching the toaster himself while it might have a live short in it."

"That's a laugh, Ed. That's a real laugh."

"You think so?"

"You're damn right. Let me spell it out for you. For the sake of argument, let's say I was desperate enough to fiddle with the thermostat. Don't you think I'd find some way to warn Hank not to go near the toaster?"

"And he'd go along with that, with setting Millie up to die? I don't think so, Al."

"So, if you don't think I did it, and if you don't think Hank would conspire with me, there are only three possible answers left."

"And they are?"

"One, that Hank did it himself. Two, that I never even worked on reassembling the toaster, and that Benson was right about me lying and covering up for Hank. And three, that it was just what Hank said it was — an accident." He grimaced. "And none of it would have happened except for your aunt Millie's greed for one lousy piece of toast."

I didn't answer him as we cut off into the airport entrance.

"Either way," Al said, "Benson won't be able to come up with anything that'll hurt either me or Hank."

I pulled into the airline terminal and stopped and kept my hands on the wheel while I stared ahead through the windshield.

"And neither will you," Al said softly.

I turned and looked at him.

"Don't try too hard at being a detective in this case, Ed," Al said. "There's no crime here."

I got out of the car and helped him get his bag out of the trunk. Al clapped me on the shoulder and gave me a hug. He stepped back and said. "It was an accident, Ed."

His eyes held mine. "Hank and I are just two old men, old friends, looking to live out our dream. Leave it at that."

I watched him as he walked away, then went back to my car and headed out of the airport and swung onto the highway back to Boston. I didn't think I'd be back up here ever again, and I wasn't even sure I'd go out to California to visit them.

I thought about a lot of things as I drove, mostly about what Al had said about them living out their dream. By the time I crossed the Vermont state line, I knew I was going to leave it at that, as Al had said. I wasn't going to probe and look for answers and keep at it until I knew everything for a certainty, one way or the other.

Maybe someday, someone — maybe Benson, or maybe even Al or Uncle Henry themselves — would turn their dream into a nightmare.

Maybe.

But it wasn't going to be me.

Tough Guy

Stephen D. Rogers

As far as I was concerned, kidnappers were the scum of the earth, not for capitalizing on the innate fears of parenthood but for causing irrevocable damage to the real victims of the crime. My kid sister was held for ransom. Twenty years later, even though payment of the demanded money long ago brought her home safely, she used a handgun to finally end her torment.

Maybe the Margolis knew my story before they hired me and maybe they didn't. They were reticent on that point. There was, however, no mistaking the fact they'd do anything to get their little girl back.

As befitting a Friday night, Margoli's was packed and the dining room was thick with the smell of authentic Italian cuisine.

Johnny was busy lapping up tonight's Sicilian Surprise. He paused every few bites to swallow, smile at me, gaze around the kingdom that was going to be ten percent his. "Is this a great place or what?"

"Been in the family for three generations. They cut their own meat, bake their own bread, grow their own herbs and spices. The pasta is made fresh daily. The Margolis know what they're doing."

"Thanks for the commercial." Johnny wiped a spot of red sauce from his shirt. "Don't get me wrong. I have no intention of getting involved with the day-to-day operations."

"You're just helping them reduce their tax obligations."

Shoveling another fork-full into his mouth, Johnny continued talking. "You know, I kind of like dealing with you instead of the family directly. It's more —" He waved his fork through the air while searching for the word. "— professional."

"When the Margolis hired me to act as go-between they had only their daughter's best interests at heart."

"I can understand that." Johnny poured himself another glass of wine and then lifted the bottle until I shook my head. "My people tell me you were a lawyer before you became a PI."

"The law wasn't my idea of justice."

Johnny sputtered, spraying the table with Chianti. "That's funny." He reached across to grab my napkin, wiped his face with the white linen before dropping it at the feet of a passing waiter. "I might be able to use someone like you in my organization."

"I could tell jokes, loosen the men up before a job."

He squinted at me as if he was trying to decide whether I was making fun of him. "What kind of money crosses your desk?"

"I get by."

Johnny shrugged, laughed to himself. "If you were so interested in money you wouldn't have gotten out of the blood-sucking racket. One time the parents sent their lawyer to act as go-between. I couldn't understand a thing he said."

"It's the Latin."

Johnny sniffed. "Lawyers and doctors. They're so important they can't even speak the same language as everybody else. Do you think Russian lawyers and Japanese doctors get away with the same bullshit?"

"I don't know."

"Yeah, you don't know, I don't know. Here's what we know." He pointed at his plate with both hands. "We're sitting at a nice restaurant enjoying a great meal. At least one of us is."

"I ate before I came."

"You said that."

"It's still true."

Johnny glanced around as if he was playing to a crowd. "It's still true. This man's too funny for his own good." He sat back and stared at me. "How much Latin you remember?"

"Brutem fulmen."

"What's that mean?"

"Inert thunder. It refers to an empty threat."

Johnny slammed back the rest of his wine. "Brute force. That's American for getting results. Speaking of results, I assume you have the signed papers."

"I'm afraid there's been a complication."

His eyes narrowed. "Now you're starting to talk like a lawyer. What complication, the Margolis don't want to see their little girl again?"

I had a sudden flash of my sister as a little girl unwrapping the doll I'd bought her with my own money. That was before she spent seventy-two hours locked in a box, before she spent years bouncing between shrinks, drugs, and the S&M scene, before the many suicide attempts, the one success.

"Before I joined you for dinner I had a little talk with your driver." I tossed a wallet into the middle of the table.

Johnny flipped through the billfold. "This is Vinny's."

Pressing the preset on my cell phone, I stalled, knowing the Margolis would take a minute to arrive. "I don't like kidnappers. My sister was kidnapped. The experience twisted her so far inside out that she finally killed herself."

"So what's with the wallet?"

"Vinny made the mistake of drawing on me. You see you were wrong before. In this matter I am not a professional. I am a wounded animal."

When Johnny glanced up, I turned enough to see the Margolis standing behind me, stern in stained aprons.

I leaned forward. "First I tried to reason with Vinny, tried to convince him to tell me where the girl was being held."

"Vinny would never tell you a thing."

"Instead, he pulled a gun and I shot him in self-defense. These people whose child you took, they turned the resulting piece of meat into Sicilian Surprise."

Johnny blanched and I thought he might vomit right then and there. Instead he only pushed his plate away. "You're insane."

"Then it's scum like you who made me that way." I paused, letting the reality of the situation sink in. I couldn't save my sister but I could save the Margolis' girl, keep Johnny from ever trying this again.

"You're one sick bastard."

"I'm not the one who ate my driver. Here's the deal. Unless the girl is returned unharmed within the next fifteen minutes, for your next meal you're going to be eating your right arm left-handed."

Johnny froze.

"I suggest you get a move on. And don't worry about your bill." I flashed my best lawyer smile. "It's on me."

Munchies

Jack Bludis

"Do you think private eyes are really like that?" Sheila said, as we filed out from a double feature of *The Maltese Falcon* and *The Big Sleep*.

"Not nearly as adventurous," I said. I looked at my watch and saw that we had plenty of time. "Let's go down Amsterdam."

"Broadway's quicker if we —"

"We can't smoke on Broadway." I was not talking about ordinary cigarettes.

I had a Minox camera in one pocket of my black designer fatigue trousers, and a Sucrets tin with a few joints and a pack of matches in the other with my keys and wallet.

"Oh," she said, and she wanted to hurry.

By the time we came to our favorite fern bar on Columbus Avenue, we had smoked half-a-joint. I was thinking about food and wine and how good it tasted when you were high on grass or hash, and about the insights that came to me. I had just left my job on Wall Street, and I thought the private eye thing might be a smart alternative.

We stepped inside, walked around to one of the long ends of the rectangular bar, and slid up on our stools. The place was something like *Cheers,* which wouldn't be on TV for a few years yet. It was only 1973, and I wasn't even thirty.

"Give us a half carafe of the red, and a plate of cheese with that special hot mustard," I said to the bartender.

"Burgundy all right?"

"Perfect."

He walked away and my mouth was watering as I thought about the cheese and wine. Wall Street was in the past, and I was still thinking about my future.

"I have the munchies," Sheila said.

"Me too," I said, and I glanced to the short sides of the bar near the front window.

"Look down there — the brunette and the surfer," I said.

"I saw them when I came in. Nice dress."

"She's married and he's not," I said.

"Nah," Sheila said. She tried to be casual as she studied the brunette in the black dress and the clean-shaven, blond guy in the Hawaiian shirt. The dress was out of sync with the wild colors most people were wearing, but it made her stand out.

"Yep. She's married," I said.

"Is that a grass insight?"

"I just know."

"You and grass," she said, and she chuckled.

The brunette caught me looking, and she smiled to herself. I didn't think the smile was about me, but more about the attention she had drawn.

The bartender brought us the cheese and he poured the wine. I tasted the wine. Then I jabbed at a hunk of cheese with a toothpick, slapped it in the mustard, and slipped it on my tongue. For some reason I thought, "Holy Communion," and I let the cheese and mustard just lay between my tongue and palate while I savored it. In a sense,

I was savoring the brunette too, because I was watching her from the corner of my eye.

"Do you think they're swingers?" Sheila said.

I shifted the cheese to the side of my jaw. "What makes you say that?"

"Just the way they look."

"You can't tell from looks." I chewed now, still savoring.

"You can tell what they are when they look at you like they want to gobble you up."

". . . And *you're* high," I added for her.

The surfer guy was looking at Sheila. The woman's smile was more overt now, and she really *was* looking at me.

"I think you nailed it," I said.

"See? I'm entitled to insights too."

I tapped the Sucrets box in the pocket of my fatigues to make sure it was there. Then I slid off the stool.

"I'll be back in a couple of minutes."

"Where you going?"

"I won't be long," I said. The brunette watched me as I walked by them and onto Columbus Avenue.

I crossed at the light, even though it was red, and walked along the shadows of 68th Street toward Central Park. I took the half-smoked joint from the tin and lit it again. I took only two hits before the euphoria enveloped me, and I wished I had brought some of the cheese. I knew what the game was, and I wanted to win at it.

When I wasn't inhaling, I cupped the joint in my palm so nobody could see it, but I took two more hits, as I came back to Columbus by way of 69th Street.

When I stepped back into the bar, the brunette and the surfer were gone from their places, and I thought I had screwed up. It was almost enough to take me down from the high.

When I looked for Sheila, she was where I left her, but now between the blond guy and the brunette who were smiling and taking turns talking. Sheila was smiling too, but there was a weakness in her smile. She was afraid, and when she saw me, she was glad I was there.

My smile wasn't real either, and the paranoia was starting to grip me. Sheila was right, they were swingers, but maybe they wanted just her.

The paranoia part of the grass high kicked in for just a second. Then it was gone. As I approached, the brunette looked at me with a smile that was not far off the Mona Lisa's, and just as puzzling.

"Ha, I'm Tracy," she said. I had expected the southern accent.

"Alan," I said.

"Like Ladd?"

"My mother's fault."

"Ah like it," she said.

"I'm Todd," said the blond guy. "And you're Alan?"

"That's what he said," Tracy said.

Now that I was there, Sheila was more comfortable, and she was smiling at Todd and rocking her leg. Her skirt had climbed well over her thigh. My chest was starting to heave under the black T-shirt. After all, I was in love with Sheila and another guy was trying to make out with her.

"Tracy says we should all go to my place," Todd said.

"Where's that?"

"55th near Sixth."

"That's not too far," I said.

Sheila looked at me.

"What do you think?" I said.

She shrugged.

My place was closer, but I had a doorman and I didn't want anybody to know about this kind of thing, even though I had never done anything like it before.

"Todd's place sounds good to me," I said.

All the cheese and mustard was gone, and I ordered a new batch to go, and the bartender wrapped it in aluminum foil and shaped it like a swan.

"Do you have wine there?" I said.

"Oh, yeah. We've got wine," Tracy said. She was high too.

I had to crunch the aluminum neck and tail of the swan to stuff it in my pocket with the Minox. Then the four of us walked over 67th, and we shared a joint as we walked along the west side of Central Park.

"What do you do?" Tracy said. She was walking with me. Sheila was with Todd.

"Wall Street," I said.

"Ooooo, sex-eee."

"It pays the bills."

"You look like an assassin in that outfit."

"Thanks."

"You like being an assassin?"

"Not yet."

She giggled and grabbed my arm as if we had known each other long enough to have a relationship.

"You want this?" Todd said, coming back to us.

Tracy let go of my arm, grabbed the joint, and sucked in hard. Todd came alongside her, and Sheila backed up, and we were back to our original pairing.

"He's cool," she said.

"Where does he keep his surfboard?"

"Jealous?" Sheila said.

"A little bit," I said.

Todd and Tracy were older than we were, and Todd seemed a little dissipated — some people just didn't know how to hold their grass.

"I'm jealous too." She grabbed my arm like Tracy had, but closer, as if she thought I would get away.

There was a lot of smoking on the streets in those days, and even if somebody minded, they didn't complain if you were discreet. Todd tossed the butt into the park. We crossed and went down Sixth Avenue, which out-of-towners still called "Avenue of the Americas." Sheila and I fell a bit behind them.

"Are you sure you want to do this?" I said.

"Don't be a party pooper." She giggled again.

"You don't have to, you know. I have a job."

"And so do I," she said. She was fully into the giggles now, and I had to stop and kiss her to cure that. Finally, she recovered.

"I want to," she said.

"What if —"

"You're being paranoid. If you want to be a private eye, why not just call it practice?" Her logic made sense.

"OK," I said.

I liked the way the black mini-dress hugged Tracy in the back, but Sheila had a better behind. Neither of the women wore a bra, so I knew that Sheila was built better too, at least to my taste.

We followed Tracy and Todd to the vestibule of a Chinese carryout on 55th Street.

"What's this all about?" My voice echoed in the small space.

"Wouldn't you like to know," Tracy said, and she giggled.

I did know though, and I thought about how I was letting a woman I *didn't* know and one I thought I might be in love with take me to something I both drooled over and feared. I also had another motive, and that seemed to make it all right, maybe even perfect.

Todd unlocked the front door and we climbed the stairs after him. Before he flicked on the lights, I thought I saw an outline of someone watching us from a window on the other side of 55th Street. It was probably part of my paranoia.

Todd's fourth-floor, front apartment was more like a large room with a kitchenette against one wall and a counter between it and the bedroom-living room area. There was a bath behind the kitchenette.

Todd took a bottle of vintage Chardonnay from a portable rack over the sink and handed it to me with a corkscrew.

"You do the honors," he said. Then he fished a professionally rolled joint from a cigar box on the counter and lit up with a stick match.

"Bring on the cheese," Tracy said.

I fumbled in my pocket to untangle the aluminum foil from the Minox.

When I put the crushed swan on the counter, Tracy went immediately domestic. She took down a serving plate from a cabinet over the sink, brought down a box of toothpicks and put it on the counter between the kitchenette and the other area. Then she rummaged through the fridge, and came up with a jar of black olives, one of green olives, and a fresh jar of mustard. Alternating between jars and the aluminum foil, she arranged everything except the bar-mustard, which she crinkled inside the foil and dropped into the plastic trash container.

"Don't you think we should close the curtains?" Sheila said.

"Shutters," Todd said, and he passed the joint to her.

Tracy was washing her hands in the sink. "Leave 'em open. Give 'em a show," she said.

She turned her head to the side, locked her gaze on mine, and she gave me that close-mouthed smile again. She continued to hold my attention while she blotted her hands on paper towels. Looking back, I think it was something like hypnotism, because from the corner of my eye, I saw

Todd and Sheila pass the joint back and forth at least twice before I broke my gaze.

Tracy stepped around the room-dividing counter and went into the big living area, where Todd and Sheila were whispering now. After Tracy stepped up to them, she turned and looked straight at me with that smile.

In what seemed like a single, long and slow motion, she reached behind her neck, untied the string, and let the dress fall. It hung at her breasts momentarily, then at her hips, and it gathered at her feet. She was totally naked underneath.

"Jesus," I said.

"Wow," Sheila said in a hoarse whisper. She stepped to the counter and held the joint in my direction. She was still holding smoke in her lungs, and she was looking at Tracy.

"Cool," Todd said.

"Now, you," Tracy said to Sheila.

I took a deep hit on the joint that was so perfectly packed and shaped that it looked as if it had been made by R.J. Reynolds.

Sheila held her breath, but she squeaked out, "Already did."

"I mean your clothes," Tracy said.

"Oh." Sheila was surprised, but I picked it up the first time.

"You don't have to," I said. I was holding my breath, but I was sure she heard me.

I watched the mustard and cheese and olives on the plate at the counter as if I thought they were going to go someplace. I had opened and poured the wine into four glasses like the ones in the bar, but I did not remember doing it.

"Why, yeah, she does," Tracy said.

"I do what?" Sheila said. She had already forgotten

what she was being asked to do, but it seemed like a long time ago.

"Take off your clothes," Tracy said.

I handed Tracy the joint, and jabbed a green olive with a toothpick on the first try. I slopped it in the mustard, and took the whole thing into my mouth. It was amazing how you could differentiate the taste of the olive and the mustard, and how good the whole thing tasted compared to when you were not high. I was concentrating on the taste and I forgot that Sheila was waiting for more reassurance.

"Oh," I said. "You don't have to."

"Don't have to what?"

"Don't have to take off your clothes."

After two tries, I jabbed a black olive, put it between my teeth, and bit down to the pit. I was gazing at Tracy, who gave the joint to Todd. She kicked her dress aside and now stood in only her platform shoes.

"Sure she has to," Todd said. He stepped behind Sheila, and cupped his hands under her breasts in the halter top. I wanted to slug him, but I knew these were the wrong circumstances for that.

"Whoa," I said, savoring the first squeeze of the black olive between my tongue and my palate where the juice was oozing. Todd stopped what he was doing, thinking I had protested. I had frightened Sheila too, but not Tracy.

"I thought you were cool with this," Tracy said.

"I am cool, but nobody asked me."

"We asked her," Todd said.

"Not really," Sheila said. She looked at me, then away, and I knew she was at least shading the truth.

Tracy stepped around the counter, went up on her toes, and touched my lips with hers. "But you *are* interested in me. And don't you tell me you are not." She was lathering on the accent.

She strolled into the big area again, making sure I saw

her behind which was better naked than under the black dress, but I still liked Sheila better. I was in love with Sheila.

I had chewed around the pit of the black olive, and I decided that I liked it better than the green one. I liked all black olives better than green olives, and all food tasted best when you had the munchies and so many things went on in your brain at the same time. I still had the Minox in my pocket, and I still had the Sucrets tin too, but it was the Minox I thought about.

"Yeah," I said.

By then, I forgot what I was answering to, and when I remembered, I realized I was saying in front of Sheila that I was interested in Tracy.

I wondered if I was kinky-sick, just kinky, or just sick. It was the times. There were a lot of deep questions whose answers we never learned, or when we learned them, we found out later that the answers were wrong, and sometimes, we just learned too late.

"Does your husband know about this?" I said.

"Not unless you tell him," Tracy said.

I wondered if she knew something that I didn't know she knew, but I decided it was just the grass that made me think that. She grabbed the joint from Sheila, who had already smoked most of it.

"Is that how private eyes do it?" Sheila squeaked out at me, still holding her breath from her last hit. I didn't know what she was talking about.

"Private eyes don't do shit," Todd said.

"Bogart does," Sheila said.

"It's just the movies," I said, and I took one each of the black and green olives and put them both in my mouth at the same time. With my other hand, I pulled out the Minox and palmed it as I palmed the joint on Central Park West.

Tracy had beckoned Sheila to her, and Sheila obeyed, and by that time, Tracy was kissing her. Sheila was reluctant at first. Then she was into it, and I clicked the Minox. Todd pulled Tracy away from Sheila as if in an adagio. When you were really high, everything seemed like a slow-motion film.

"You do him. I do her," Todd said.

"He won't cooperate," Tracy cooed, but she decided to try again. She took two long strides and stepped to my side of the counter. Her breasts were small, with a small bounce, but they were shaped well.

I wanted to, damn, did I want to. I could blame it on the grass, and the fact that I had been away from my job on Wall Street for almost a month now. I could claim I didn't know what I was doing.

Tracy was naked, but I still wore my big-pocket fatigue pants and my black T-shirt, and Todd was running his hand under Sheila's mini. I was out of sync with the others, but in sync with the situation, because I still knew what I had to do. I understood food and people and my life and its meaning and everything else there was to know. Everything I needed was here, but some of it was in my mind.

"Do you like blondes or brunettes better?" Tracy said.

"Blondes," I said. I tried not to watch Sheila and Todd.

"Ah you tryin' to hurt my feelin's?" Tracy said. She was exaggerating her Virginia accent to the point of parody.

"Not at all," I said.

I could actually tell which bits were green olive and which were black. I liked the texture and the shape of the pit, but I liked the taste of the black olives best. I liked blondes better than brunettes, I liked Sheila better than Tracy, and I wished I had bought an apple coming down Broadway.

I was trying not to watch, but I saw how Todd was examining Sheila's tonsils with his tongue, and she was fully into it.

"Let's go," I said across the room to Sheila, but she was busy.

"Have you tried a brunette lately?" Tracy said. Her hard nipples touched me through the 100% cotton of my T-shirt, and she kissed me again. Her tongue slipped from between her lips. For just a fraction of a second, I reacted. Then I backed away.

"No," I said.

"You heard Todd — I do you and he does Sheila. It's the only fair way."

"Come on, Sheila, let's go."

"You go," Sheila said, breaking her oral entanglement for just a moment. Her halter-top was loose, but I focused my attention on the front of her skirt, which bulged from Todd's hand.

"I assure you, I'm very good," Tracy said.

"I like Sheila," I said.

I felt stupid, especially because I was watching Sheila and Todd and I was excited by Tracy, but I was thinking about olives all at the same time.

"I like her too," Tracy said, and she went over to where Todd was kissing Sheila. She lifted up Sheila's skirt and I saw where Todd's hand was.

"Nice," Tracy said.

I was jealous, but I was excited too. "Let's go," I said. I was trying to be forceful, but my voice was cracking.

"Mmmmm," Sheila moaned at Todd. Then she said, "Go without me," and she said it with conviction.

"OK," I said, and now my excitement had risen to anger, and I took another shot with the Minox, as Tracy reached around the front of Sheila and peeled away her halter top.

I picked up one of the black olives with my fingers, and I put it in my mouth, and I watched them move in slow motion. I watched clothes, and mouths and hands and other body parts. By the time I ate two more olives, Todd had opened up the sofa bed, and all three of them were naked and entangled on what looked like satin sheets. I raised the Minox next to the plate, and took two more shots.

"This is . . . ooooo." Sheila moaned and for just a moment, I thought she was talking about the olives, because they were so good, but it was me who was totally out of it, me who didn't understand.

"Take off your clothes," Tracy said across the room to me. I was still behind the counter.

I took two more shots with the Minox, and I raised it to eye level because I wanted to make sure I got everybody in the picture. Tracy looked up and I got her full face, with most of her body. The others were behind her. She saw what I was doing, but I didn't care. I took one more good photo, moved toward the door, and unbolted the lock.

"Hey!" Tracy called from the sofa bed, and she scrambled to her feet, but Sheila was too occupied to notice.

I was on my way down the worn linoleum stairs and Tracy was on the landing above me, and she was naked. "Hey," she called again.

By the time I had turned the latch on the front door, I could no longer see her. I heard her coming down the stairs, but she did not follow me onto the street.

Spade would never do that and Marlowe would never do it, but it was what being a private eye was all about — finding things and finding people, and maybe more importantly, finding out about people.

I was being paid to find out about Tracy, but what I learned about Sheila was a bonus. Learning about myself was a bonus too, but I still don't know why I didn't join them. Maybe the old Catholic in me wasn't totally gone yet, or maybe I thought my testimony would be no good in the divorce if I went through with it. I had a new job and a new reputation to build and maybe even one to protect.

The next time I saw an image of Tracy Gallagher, was in the black-and-white, front-page photo in the *Daily News.* She lay on a carpet someplace, and there was black blood all down the front of her white dress.

I ended up testifying for the defense at her husband's murder trial. He had a sharp lawyer who had worked the jury for extenuating circumstances. I should have been happy with that, but I wasn't, because it was my report and my photos that drove him over the edge. If there was guilt, I shared it, and I wanted them to tell me that.

One thing I do know now is that I like black olives better than green. There was one other insight too — the Sheila thing — but I still don't know if that was good or bad.

The best thing that came out of it, I suppose, was that it was my first job as a PI, and I earned an immediate reputation for getting things done.

Gourmet Takeout

Art Montague

Mickey Scharfe usually defended mob guys, which explained his $3,000 suits, his custom made shirts, and the mistress he had tucked away in a Caledon Hills mansion.

Joey Ganzer worked on and off for Mickey as his investigator. Mickey was known as poor pay and slow pay, which explained Ganzer's off-the-rack suits, his drip-dry shirts, and the hangdog look of a middle-aged man who wasn't getting enough and probably never would. Ganzer had no investigator's license. He'd never applied, knowing it wouldn't be approved anyway. Yet, the police let him do his work. Maybe they liked his style; maybe he was doing things they wished they could be doing.

Ganzer was ex-Seal, ex-cop. Perhaps he was an American. On the other hand, some Canadians enlisted to fight other people's wars because Canada had none of its own. No one ever asked him how he came to live in Toronto. His looks didn't invite questions. His feline eyes never shared his smile and his smile was hardly ever kindly.

But Ganzer could get into places where Mickey and often the mob guys feared to tread, which was why Mickey liked his work and called him whenever such visits had to happen. Mickey never asked him what he did with his time when he wasn't on the Scharfe clock. He didn't want to know, not that Ganzer would have told him. More likely the investigator would have shrugged off the question, replying, "I pay the rent."

When the Reese case came down the pipe, Mickey set a meeting with Ganzer for after six, giving the legal secretaries and clerks time to leave the office. Ganzer assumed the odd hour meant the case was a little edgy. Either that or Mickey thought Ganzer's Wal-Mart wardrobe and aura of latent aggression would downgrade his elegant office ambience or make the staff nervous.

The two men settled in Mickey's inner office with rye to the brim in heavy old-fashioned glasses.

"Joey, I've taken a client that isn't our usual. I wouldn't have touched it, but the price was right." He paused to sip his drink. Mickey always liked talking about money, especially his own. "Plus my instincts tell me this one is innocent."

"That's something new," replied Ganzer. "Innocent of the beef or innocent period?" Ganzer liked clarity as much as Mickey liked smoke and mirrors.

"Both."

Something to think about. "You losing weight, Mickey?"

"No, why?"

"The braces."

Mickey looked down. "Suspenders. I figure if they work for Larry King, they'll work for me. Image." He smiled like Ganzer wouldn't have a clue what image was.

Ganzer needled a little. "So who's Larry King?" Mickey took himself far too seriously. Ganzer learned to ignore mirrors years ago.

"Doesn't matter," said Mickey, ruffled. He recovered fast, that lawyer persona clicking up like a Teflon shield.

"I've put together a case file you can take with you."

"How about the highlights now?" Ganzer stood and helped himself to Mickey's rye.

"In a nutshell. The client and his wife are on their way to a special anniversary dinner. A mugger puts it to them in an underground parking garage, shoots her, pistol-whips him, gets the wallet, purse, jewelry. Okay so far?"

"You've taken a mugger for a client?"

Mickey waved off the question. "Two days later the mugger's picked up trying to peddle the jewelry in a Queen Street pawnshop." Ganzer waited for the other shoe.

"The mugger decides he wants to plead down, which suits the police just fine so long as the story jibes with the theory they like."

"The husband set it up," said Ganzer.

"How'd you know?"

"Muggers can't afford your fees."

Mickey continued. "Seems there's a divorce in the works, lots of insurance, an affair on the wife's side. Motive, opportunity, maybe the means, too, if it's a contract. The mugger says it's a contract. Bingo, I have a client."

"How much?"

"That's confidential."

"Mickey, I don't care about your fees. The hit, how much?"

"Seventy-five thousand total, maybe ten of it up front confirmed, at least on Reese's end. The mugger says he never saw a nickel up front. Says my client welshed."

"Maybe your client was waiting for an invoice."

"Very funny."

"I try. Anyway, that helps. What else? I presume you want the mugger's story broken."

"Right."

"This isn't your usual, Mickey. It doesn't sound like mine, either."

"The client's Colin Reese."

"I guessed that — I saw it on the news. I always watch the local after Larry King. Real estate, buy cheap, gentrify, sell high. Where do I come in?"

"The mugger is Eddie Boccarri's fifty-two year old uncle. Still, I think it was a straight mugging."

"This uncle connected?"

"Never. Too low for that. So's Eddie for that matter. Neither one could even make it as a wannabe."

"So that's my job?"

"You know the rocks to turn over."

"That I do." Ganzer picked up the file and stood. "I'll get back to you, Mickey."

At the door Ganzer paused and turned. "Why do you feel good about this one?"

"Reese and his wife fancied themselves gourmets. They were on their way to a special dinner Reese had orchestrated ahead of time. Reese wouldn't have wanted to miss it. He'd have scheduled the hit for after they'd eaten."

Ganzer smiled at that. "I guess you know your people. I'll want to talk to him."

"Done. Anything else, call."

The gourmet dinner stuck in Ganzer's mind. He'd never been exposed to anything that might pass as gourmet food. Takeouts and frozen dinners he could wing into his microwave were his grub *du jour.* When he was on per diem for meals, he'd sometimes eat at budget family restaurants; upscale dining was way beyond Mickey's allowance. Ganzer decided he needed a little handle on this so-called gourmet dinner in an exclusive restaurant. First, however, he decided to walk on more familiar turf: Eddie Boccarri's.

The Trattoria del Roma didn't even serve meals — unless takeout from the spaghetti palace next door counted. The joint was a mildewed basement card room on Bloor Street. It offered yesterday's coffee or the watered-down booze regulars knew was secreted below the bar. The place was a hangout for also-rans, has-beens, and, worse, people who thought they could still get some action on.

That last bunch, they were dangerous. Eddie Boccarri was one of them. His package was a long track record of near misses and screw-ups that usually ended with someone hurt and someone else doing time. Failures had made him vicious and experience had made him cunning. His genes were probably responsible for his stupidity. The worst kind of stupid — he thought he was smart.

Eddie was always heeled. His cunning dictated that his girlfriend carry for him, usually in her purse placed conspicuously within his easy reach.

Stupid? Anyone who knew anything about Eddie — and Ganzer did — knew that the time to hit him was when his girlfriend was in the john. What woman doesn't take her purse to the john? So, Ganzer simply waited.

By the time she finished having a leak and snorting a line of Eddie's coke, Ganzer had Eddie out in the alley slumped against a Dumpster. None of the customers had lifted an eyebrow when Ganzer made his move. Some already knew Ganzer, knew to stay out of it. The others figured it was Eddie's beef and they didn't owe him squat.

"We needed some privacy, Eddie," said Ganzer, kicking him hard in the ribs. He heard a rib crack over Eddie's whimpering. Steel-toed brogues can do that.

"Now I have your attention, now we can talk. I need to know some things."

"I got nothing that would do you any good," Eddie gasped, apparently in some pain but still way too feisty.

Ganzer kicked him again, hearing another of those distinctive cracks. He could see Eddie's compliance level climb as his body tried to curl around the pain.

"That's better," said Ganzer. "If you hurt in more than one place, the hurts neutralize each other. Except maybe for a kick in the balls, which may be coming next. Tell me about your uncle's beef. I heard you had a piece of it."

"Nothing to do with it. Guido was on his own."

"What else, Eddie?" asked Ganzer, ominously.

"OK, I sold him the gun. It was hot anyway. Fired in the liquor store job. Guido didn't know any better."

"What about Reese? How'd a mope like Guido meet an uptown guy like Reese?"

"No idea, man. I need a doctor. You didn't need to do this to me."

"Yeah, yeah, I did, Eddie. A mood comes over me, Ganzer said. "Now I don't want to come back to you, Eddie. So just to be sure I have everything, tell me, when did you sell Guido the gun?"

"A week or so before the score. I didn't know what he was going to do."

Ganzer took a step back from Eddie. "You really don't know much, Eddie, but I suppose I should thank you for your help. Go now. Get your ribs taped, and get a splint on that broken thumb. Your nose'll be OK. It'll just hurt for a while. Could have been worse. Might still be. See you around." With that, Ganzer walked off down the alley.

Café Jules was the contrast to the Trattoria that Ganzer had expected. Linen tablecloths, crystal glasses, heavy silver cutlery, dark damask tapestries on the walls: food was ritual here. Orders would be whispered or conveyed with nods or dainty regal finger flicks. A basin of holy water by the reception lectern would not have surprised Ganzer.

It was four o'clock. Ganzer didn't want customers dividing the time of the owner when they had their little tête à tête.

Jules Brisson was the name Mickey had supplied. The man with the name was short and fat — not stocky fat that comes with a welfare diet but stocky fat that comes with rich sauces and prime cuts. The look on his face when Ganzer introduced himself suggested he'd prefer Ganzer use the service entrance if he came back. He didn't exactly sniff but his disdain was apparent. Ganzer chose to ignore it for the time being.

"The police have already interviewed me, Mr. Ganzer," he said. "I can't fathom that I could possibly add anymore information than I have already provided."

"That may be, but I prefer to hear things fresh. Like your food, fresh is best."

"Oh my, yes. We insist on that quality. It's our reputation. That, and culinary artistry."

Ganzer had struck a chord. "The dinner for the Reeses must have been an achievement."

"Indeed, but, sadly, lost. The fruits of a month-long collaboration between Mr. Reese and myself. A renowned saucier brought here specially from Nice to finish the *boucheé* of escargots and Morel mushrooms. He was to prepare the cream sauce — cognac with roasted garlic, garnished with organic chives we cultivate in our own rooftop greenhouse. I'm sorry, I digress, but the thought of it, you understand . . ."

"I do," said Ganzer. Probably as good as getting a free pizza because the guaranteed delivery was late. "Were there any other noteworthy items on the menu?"

"Everything, Mr. Ganzer. Every detail. The red-hued ice sculpture, the folds of its open rose petals cradling

Beluga caviar, live Swedish crayfish flown in to be cooked at table. Oazacan radishes carved into shapes of two lovers — somewhat erotic for my tastes — but in some respects Mr. Reese could be insistent. The small points, you understand; the framing of the art, but not its creation."

"The menu sounds international."

"You've captured the concept almost exactly. Mr. Reese strived to provide his wife's favorite dishes from places they'd visited throughout the world. Many ingredients had to be flown in to ensure freshness and authenticity.

"The variety for the special occasion notwithstanding, Mrs. Reese was as discerning and demanding a gourmet as Mr. Reese, rarely shared qualities in a couple, I'm sure you'll agree.

"I've prepared food for the powerful and the wealthy, Mr. Ganzer, even for royals. Most are indifferent to their food. They chatter inconsequentials as they fill their bellies. They insult me!

"Mr. Reese and his wife? Ah, their conversation during dinner was always about the dinner, never the nonsense of the Dow Jones index or next month's ski conditions at Whistler or Aspen or St. Moritz. The Reeses knew ambrosia when it touched their palates."

"This was a month in the planning?" asked Ganzer.

"Easily that. I could look at my calendar to confirm, but I would say Mr. Reese and I chatted about it many times before he gave the go-ahead. A trip around the world in one meal. That's what he wanted for his wife."

"No expense spared? Is that about it?"

"You do understand this was to have been a priceless experience?" Ganzer nodded tolerantly from time to time as Brisson explained.

"Mr. Reese handled travel and shipping costs separately. I would guess several thousands for those. The bill from here was of course much less, given the circumstances. Wines and gratuities were not an issue. Consultations with me, preparation work, the embarrassment to me of having a professional photographer on hand with nothing to photograph, to say nothing of two local food critics. My bill was under $4,000."

"He paid?"

"But certainly. Mr. Reese is a gentleman as well as a businessman. He understands such things."

When he finished with Brisson, Ganzer wasn't the least bit hungry. He called Mickey from the restaurant to confirm clearance to visit Reese at the Remand Center.

Even in jailhouse khakis, Reese projected a well-fed patrician image. The Remand Center hadn't caved him. The man projected alertness and confidence, so much so that Ganzer had the thought he might have been here before or knew how to acclimatize as quick as a chameleon changes color. *First impression, probably wrong.* What Ganzer realized he was looking at was power and polish. Reese was probably getting daily facials and manicures from the queens.

So far, Ganzer's jury of one just man — himself — was still out on Reese. The big question seemed to be how Reese could have hooked up with Guido. Even Eddie Boccarri hadn't been able to answer that one.

"Jules Brisson sends his regards," Ganzer began. "So does Mickey. I came from Mickey."

"What about my bail?" asked Reese. He had his own priorities.

"Not my job. I think he has a paralegal working on it."

"What *is* your job?"

"A little this, a little that. I do background, which is why I'm here. I need to hear your side of it from the top."

Reese was keen on eye contact. Ganzer didn't mind. Let the wheels turn; eventually they'd stop, because at this moment Ganzer was the only one Reese had to talk to.

The "gentleman and businessman" finally looked away. In the first ten minutes he was trying like hell to be the aggrieved innocent and generally doing pretty well, except every now and then the calculating wheeler-dealer side of him came through like an exterminator at a flea circus.

"We were on our way to reconciliation — slowly, but I was hopeful. By that point in our relationship, food was about the only thing we could still agree on. With the anniversary coming up, the dinner was a natural."

"The police say she was having an affair."

"I knew about it, and she knew I did. We never discussed it and the man left town."

"Did you help him along?"

"Ten grand worth."

"So that was the cash withdrawal you made a couple of weeks before the incident?"

"Right. I told the police that."

"The boyfriend denied it. I don't suppose you have a receipt?" asked Ganzer.

"Are you being funny? Because this isn't funny. Does Scharfe keep you around for your wit?"

"Nope, he keeps me around to solve problems of people who talk too much to the police, among other things," Ganzer said. "Did you pay the money directly to the guy or did you use it to hire someone to help him along? Ten grand doesn't seem like a lot of incentive, given your wife could have offered more if she figured he was a keeper."

"Directly, Ganzer. Some people come cheaper than others."

"Sure, but sometimes you only get what you pay for." Ganzer paused. "Like Guido."

"Screw you, Ganzer. I never met this Guido. I never did a deal with him. Let's back up — who in hell are you working for? Me. I'm paying the bills. So don't screw me around." Reese was shouting.

Very evenly, Ganzer replied. "Mr. Reese, I don't work for you. I work for Mickey Scharfe. Part of my work is to find out everything about a case that his client didn't tell him. Mickey hates courtroom surprises. So do I, because when it happens, Mickey gets on my ass.

"Now, let's continue. Who was driving that night, you or your wife? And why choose a parking garage three blocks from the restaurant when there's half a dozen closer?"

Reese glared. "I drove, as you probably know. I had tickets for a concert after dinner. I parked half a block from the concert hall, assuming we'd be tired by the time it was over and wouldn't want to walk far to the car. Nor may you be aware, a walk before dinner stimulates the appetite. I wanted Diana primed. What else?"

"Tell me about this dinner."

Reese's demeanor changed. He smiled, sat up straighter. His pupils dilated, as if he'd just mainlined a cap of the best.

Damn, thought Ganzer, *another Jules.* He listened patiently, wondering, as Reese rolled through the menu, how Remand Center slop on a tin tray went down for him.

The last thing Reese gave Ganzer was the name of the boyfriend. Not for a second did he think the guy had left town. Reese also came up with the name of the place where the guy had worked as a personal trainer: Brad Winters, and he'd worked for Fitness Foremost.

Ganzer still needed two days to track him down. He dropped over to Fitness Foremost but didn't even bother going in. The joint obviously specialized in outcalls, and fitness was definitely not foremost among its services. That explained why $10,000 may have been enough for a buy-off.

Ganzer was puzzled that the missus would use a place

so sleazy. The Yellow Pages gave him the reason: a tasteful full-page ad offering everything from in-home aerobic programs and massages to yoga, Reikian therapy, and colonic irrigation. Ganzer guessed that if a customer never saw the joint they'd never be the wiser.

Only after Ganzer went around and around with a dozen other so-called health clubs and fitness centers did he find Winters, still working out of Fitness Foremost, only now he was Brad Summers. Ganzer was angry for not tumbling quicker to this apparent man for all seasons. He wasn't quite so when Ganzer was done with him. There wasn't much spring left in his step, something a sudden fall can do.

Winters denied the payoff. At first. Then he admitted he'd taken it. Why had he denied it to the police? Simple. If his boss heard about it, he would have demanded a piece. But, yes, he would now testify to the truth.

On the other hand, Winters admitted he was still providing services to the missus as recently as two days before the murder. They were in love, he said. That muddied the water, but Reese seemed convinced the payoff had done the job. Even the sharpest guy can be wrong.

Mickey was pressing. He'd gone for an early trial date and wanted a final word from Ganzer.

The bottom line so far was that, except for Guido's word, the evidence was circumstantial. Reese and Guido could not be connected.

Then there was Ganzer's take, which he reported to Mickey: "Reese spent a fortune on the meal. I saw his eyes; he'd have eaten before a hit. You were bang on with that theory, Mickey.

"So for facts, you've got a few you can work. First, Reese paid off the boyfriend. If he was going to whack his wife, he would have saved his money.

"Second, and for this you didn't need me," said Ganzer, "all you had to do was look at a calendar. Reese was planning his dinner two weeks before Guido claims they even met. Does a guy make an investment like that without knowing yet if he can really buy everything he wants? Reese has never done a deal that crapped out. He always knows his bottom line. Goes to show he didn't need the insurance either.

"The last thing is Guido pawning the jewelry. Sure, Reese may have welshed but more likely Guido was just doing what muggers do when they have hot jewelry."

"So, Guido all the way?" asked Mickey. "That's what you're telling me?"

"You know it. Random. But Mickey, be careful on this one. I still don't feel right. If I had more time, maybe I could put my finger on it. I think the cops should have looked deeper. My guess is they assume some innuendo and loose testimony will be enough. Reese may think he's refined but he still comes across as street slick. The jury will see that and the cops know it. Anyway, not my problem. Not yours either. I'll send you my bill."

Ganzer was by no means a neatness freak, but he hated being conned. The trial came and went. Needless to say, Guido went down. Hell, he copped a plea for testimony; his fate was foregone. Reese walked. Guido's testimony was so self-serving no jury in the world would believe it, especially after a Mickey Scharfe cross-examination, and despite Reese being an obvious jerk.

In his spare time Ganzer plugged along. He went deep; he went very deep. He tracked Reese back practically to the womb, same for his wife, same for Guido and Eddie. When Mickey suggested he cool it because the street was getting uptight, he gave some thought to checking him out as well. He cozied up to some people — not easy for him — cajoled others, and crowded the rest. He cashed a few favors, but not many. Mostly he crowded.

Came a time when he decided Eddie needed another visit, but he missed him by a day. Eddie was dead. That was as useful as anything Eddie could have said.

Ganzer figured he finally had all of the pieces. Now he could resolve the issue of his pride. He paid Reese a visit.

"Scharfe's been paid in full, Ganzer. What do you want?"

"You and Mickey were in a bit of a hurry, so I didn't really have time to do the kind of job I prefer. Now I have, so I thought I'd drop by and give you a report."

"It's over with, Ganzer."

"Double jeopardy for the wife, right you are. Anyway, sit down, shut up for a minute.

"As for Guido, the stupid schmuck, your connection went right back to stickball days in the West End and continued through the years when you used to be just another young rounder on the make for a good score. You finally found that, which is where you got the seed money to get into real estate. That's also when you met your wife, and, with her holding these youthful indiscretions over your head, you'd have taken a supreme bath in divorce court, which is exactly where you knew you were headed. Good so far?"

"Get out of here!" Reese sprang from his chair and started moving around the corner of his desk. Like flicking away a fly, Ganzer backhanded him across the mouth, hard enough for some blood spray. Reese stumbled back to his chair.

"That was a rhetorical question. Now, you could have reached out for a pro to look after your problem but you knew the polish would show. So you looked up Guido, who was doing the same penny ante scores as when you left the West End umpteen years ago. No big deal, you've always known where to look — you could get there on the subway in ten minutes. I bet he jumped at the chance to make the big time.

"I read in the paper Eddie Boccarri's dead. The paper said it was a pro hit. He was related to your wife, third or fourth cousin, right? Small world. She's gone. He's gone, maybe insurance against the off chance he might remember the old days, or more likely Eddie did remember and figured his silence was worth something to you. No double jeopardy on him. Still, there's Guido. If Eddie's related, maybe Guido is, too. How long before he gets shanked in the yard?"

"Get to the point, Ganzer." Reese was dabbing tissue at the corner of his mouth.

Ganzer shrugged. "No point. No payoff. I do what I'm asked to do. Mickey pays my bill. End of case.

"One thing, though," continued Ganzer. "There's still a puzzle. Why waste the dinner?"

"You should have spent more time talking to Jules Brisson. The dinner was everything Diana loved."

"He did mention something like that, but probably by then my stomach was turning."

"The only way to get her to go was to make the menu irresistible. My personal tastes are different, far more refined. If I'd had to eat that dinner, I'd have been in the can ten minutes later hanging over a toilet bowl with my finger down my throat."

"Me too," Ganzer agreed. Reese laughed, dribbling some blood, but Ganzer didn't. He had been serious.

"'Nuff said, Reese, I'm on my way. In case you're thinking of reaching out like you did for Eddie, I just taped our chat and in half an hour it'll be in a safe place unless, of course, I get mugged on the way. Neither of us would like that to happen. Ever."

Reese sat for a time, staring at the door. He thought about a lot of things, but not once did it enter his head to pick up the phone. Ever.

Mimosa

Carol Kilgore

Ah, Miami! The best city in the world, and Victor Obregon's hometown. Victor walked into the Plaza Cubano, a dance club on Miami Beach, shortly before midnight and watched the dance floor from the shadows of the bar.

Men strutted like peacocks, showing off for the women. And what women they were. Some beautiful, some not so, all with the same longing in their eyes. Victor loved women, and he would strut, too . . . if he wasn't working.

A redhead walked up to him and smiled. "Dance?"

Any other night he would have been eager to do so. He caressed her arm. "Not tonight. Perhaps another time."

She shrugged and returned to her table. Victor ran his fingers through his short, freshly clipped hair then shot his cuffs. The tic beneath his right eye jumped. Time to earn his money.

The woman he was here to see stood out from all the rest, as if a spotlight shone on her. Her long black hair hung in curls almost to her waist, and the red dress fit her as if she had been sewn into it, its low-cut bodice revealing a promise of more. She stood at the far end of the bar holding a drink. That was how he knew her — a Latin beauty in a red dress with a drink to match her name — Mimosa.

Her body was perfect, the kind every man yearned to possess, all the way to the tips of her toes in the high-heeled sandals she wore. Tonight she would belong to him. Only not in the way most men would prefer.

Victor was here on PI business. His client, a Coconut Grove accountant named Armando Cruz, said he was with Mimosa at the time his partner was murdered. Victor's job was to get Mimosa to confirm his statement. Armando had not told the police of his alibi, because he didn't want his wife to know. That was all right . . . Victor could spend the money of a stupid man as easily as the money of a smart one.

Armando said Mimosa showed up at the Plaza Cubano late every Saturday night. She always ordered a Mimosa and a cup of orange sections. Victor watched her. One by one, she dipped the sections into the orange juice and champagne concoction before running her tongue over each of them, then placing them in her mouth. It was a sight to behold. He sighed.

The bandleader announced the mambo contest — Victor loved the mambo. He especially loved dancing it with a sexy woman, and Mimosa was the sexiest in the club. He walked to her, held out his hand. Her gaze traveled from his face to his feet, then back up again, pausing briefly on the way. She smiled, placed her hand in his. Victor led her to the dance floor, secure in the knowledge women found him irresistible.

On the floor, he drew her to him. "Victor," he said.

Her steamy gaze wandered over his face. Victor watched in fascination as she parted her lips and brushed her tongue across the tips of her teeth. No wonder Armando had fallen under her spell.

He stood as still as a statue waiting for the music to begin, not wanting the moment to end. Blood roared in his ears, and he barely heard her whisper her name.

"Mimosa." The word caressed his soul and created a tingle in his spine. The faint scent of oranges followed her smile.

Horns blasted the first torrid notes, and he stepped into the dance, leading Mimosa into an opening spin. They moved perfectly together, attuned on more than a physical level. He slid his hand lower down her back, and she gasped.

The music flowed within Victor, and he led Mimosa through intricate, seductive moves. She followed seamlessly, as if they had practiced together for years. They moved as one. His skin tingled where they touched, and he longed to possess her.

Only three couples remained on the dance floor. The music grew more fervent. Two couples remained. He saw the judge touch the other couple and ask them to leave. He and Mimosa had won. The music ended, the judge presented them to the crowd and handed each of them a fifty-dollar bill. Applause and shouts of "More!" rained down on them. They were asked to start the next dance, and at Mimosa's nod, Victor eagerly complied.

After they finished the dance, he led Mimosa back to the bar. With a crisp new U.S. Grant in his pocket, he ordered her a fresh drink and himself an Absolut on the rocks.

"Tell me about yourself, Mimosa." She was as beautiful up close as from a distance, maybe more so. Her eyes were a startling blue.

Mimosa shrugged. "There is not much to tell. My parents brought me from Cuba when I was only three years old. This is the country I know, yet my heart beats with this music. The music of my soul."

Victor understood about the music, even though his own parents had been born in Miami. But he wasn't here to talk about the music or about being Cuban. "Do you come here often?"

"Yes, each Saturday night, for a few months now. I love to dance." She smiled and touched his cheek. "Especially with handsome men."

"You're a very good dancer." He ran his fingers along the back of her hand.

"Never before have I won the mambo contest. Thank you." She took back her hand, looked down at the bar, then plucked an orange section from the clear plastic cup, dunked it into her drink, then raised it to her lips.

"May I ask you a question?" He wanted to get business out of the way so he could concentrate on Mimosa. Perhaps tonight would be beneficial for him in more ways than one.

She nodded and slipped the fruit into her mouth, her tongue licking the juice from the corner of her full red lips.

Victor pried his gaze from her. He reached into his jacket pocket, pulled out a photograph of Armando Cruz, and slid it across the table. "Do you recognize him?"

Mimosa picked up the photograph. Victor watched her. He thought a shadow flickered across her face, but it passed so quickly he couldn't be sure.

She handed the photograph back to him, and looked into his eyes then quickly away. "No, I do not recognize this man."

Victor pocketed his hope. "You've never seen him? Never danced with him . . . here, at the Plaza Cubano?"

"No. Never." She sipped her drink, then looked at him from beneath her eyelashes. "May we dance again?"

"Of course." He downed his vodka. He would enjoy the music once more with Mimosa in his arms.

After that dance, Victor walked Mimosa back to the bar, then left the dance club. He pulled his car, a nondescript white Honda, out of the parking lot to a place on the street where he could watch the club's entrance. He waited for Mimosa to exit.

She had been stiff on the last dance. No one watching would have known, but he had felt it in her muscles and in the way she followed his lead. Because of that, he knew he had been correct about the shadow clouding her face when she looked at Armando's photograph. Mimosa had lied.

He expected her to give him time to leave, then leave herself. That didn't happen. It was well past two when she left the club. Alone.

She passed the parking lot and walked up Ocean Drive . . . north, toward Second Street. Victor's car faced the opposite direction, so he turned and watched through the back window. Mimosa crossed the intersection and kept going — time to move.

Even at two in the morning, Ocean Drive traffic continued to roll lightly. He caught a break with the traffic signals, pulled out and made a U-turn, barely missing a group of inebriated young men crossing in mid-block. One mooned him, and the others issued taunts to do the physically impossible. He drove slowly past.

A block ahead, Mimosa crossed Third Street, still walking north on Ocean. He stopped at the still-green light and turned on his flashers. The driver of the car behind him flipped him the finger as he passed. The light turned red, and Victor turned off his flashers. At this time of night, he could do the same thing at each block without a large risk.

Mimosa turned on Fourth, and Victor received his first

good glimpse of her as she passed under the glow of the streetlights. He had been afraid she had tricked him, exchanging clothes and having someone else wear her dress out of the club. But this was definitely Mimosa. No other woman had the same seductive swing to her hips.

He sat at the light on Ocean, and his gaze traveled down the length of her body. Below her short skirt were the taut leg muscles of a dancer or runner — someone accustomed to exercising those muscles every day. Below those leg muscles were feet shoved into the highest stiletto heels he had ever seen. He had not been aware of their height at the club. How had she danced as she did with those on? And how had she walked three — going on four — blocks balancing on those stiletto points?

Mimosa crossed the intersection and walked toward Collins Avenue. Victor turned on to Fourth, staying a block behind. Damn! Mimosa turned up a short sidewalk. He looked for an open parking place, but both sides of the street were full.

He had no choice but to drive ahead. As he neared the private sidewalk, he saw a small stucco house between two buildings. It was white, set back in a tiny yard filled with hibiscus and lemon trees. A low iron fence surrounded the property, and a small flock of pink plastic flamingos guarded a birdbath filled with colored glass balls.

Mimosa let herself inside and closed the door as he passed. An empty parking space loomed at the corner, but he couldn't chance parking there. Mimosa may have been aware of his car and be watching from a darkened window.

He continued straight, parked in the next block, then walked back toward the little house past a Cuban grocery and a hat shop. At the corner something hard poked him in the back. A pair of hands slammed him into the building.

A male voice with a Cuban accent whispered in his ear, "Mimosa is not yours. *¡Veta a la chingada!*"

A fist rammed into his right kidney. Again. Then again. When his cheek hit the concrete, he slid into a black cloud.

Victor awoke to the gray luster of dawn and his cheek in a puddle of drool. He groaned and pushed himself off the sidewalk. Nausea struck immediately, but he hobbled to the curb before throwing up. A big yellow tabby watched from across the street, its orange eyes conveying disdain for all things human. Victor wondered if a hair ball felt this bad. After a few minutes, he supported his weight against a streetlight, regained his balance, then staggered to his car.

Before opening the door, he leaned his forehead against the cool metal of the roof and stood like that for a few minutes. The fog in his brain slowly lifted, and his thoughts centered on one question — what had he stumbled into?

Victor grabbed two bottles — Absolut from the freezer and Advil from the kitchen counter — then headed to the bathroom. He relaxed against the back of his old clawfoot tub, never letting the water cool. He had long ago mastered the art of controlling the knobs with his feet. By the time he looked like a Cuban prune, the pain was bearable and he had a plan.

Logic said he should confront his client with what had happened and demand the truth, or he should walk away from the case, but Victor had never been one to listen to logic. So he applied a small bandage to the cut on his cheek, dressed in a soft cotton shirt and loose pants, careful to avoid the large bruise on his back, and drove back to Mimosa's house.

He parked right in front, strolled up the walk, and rang the bell. No answer. He rang it again, this time punching it repeatedly.

"One moment," came a muffled voice from inside. The door opened a few inches, secured by a chain, and Mimosa's eyes widened when she saw him.

"Let me in," Victor said, steel in his voice.

Mimosa nodded, released the chain, and let him enter.

Inside the darkened room, Victor's eyes adjusted to the change in light. After his vision returned, he saw that Mimosa wore a faded flannel robe and her feet were bare. Desire to run his fingers through her sleep-mussed hair overcame him, and he fisted his hands to keep from following through.

"Please, have a seat. What happened to your face?" She motioned toward a pink sectional sofa.

Victor sat. "A small cut."

"Would you like coffee or orange juice?"

"No, thank you. Nothing. I came to talk to you."

"May I get dressed? It won't take but a minute."

"Go ahead." He hoped she wouldn't climb out a window. He walked around the small room, alert for any odd sound.

True to her word, Mimosa came back within a few minutes. She wore white shorts and a red halter top. Her long hair was pulled back and held with a red plastic clip. Without makeup, she was more beautiful than the night before. Her blue eyes shone clear in the soft light.

"What is it you want?" she asked.

"I think you know."

She sighed and sank into a chair. "Armando."

Bingo! "Yes, Armando. Why didn't you tell me about him last night when I asked?"

"I was afraid." She looked at the floor.

"Why?" He watched dust motes dance in a skinny

sliver of sunlight creeping across the floor. He should be watching Mimosa, but he wanted to concentrate on her voice, not her beauty.

"Because I heard about what happened." She took a deep breath. "I heard about his partner's murder, that Armando had been arrested. And I heard about Armando's wife."

He looked up at her, searched her eyes.

"I did not know he was married. I thought perhaps his wife had sent you." She glanced away.

"His wife didn't send me. He did. My name is Victor Obregon, and I'm a private investigator. Did he tell you anything that night, or before? Anything that might lead you to believe he was involved in the murder?"

"No, nothing." She shook her head.

"Did he indicate any resentment or anger toward his partner?"

"No! He never mentioned him at all. He just told me he was an accountant."

"How about clients? Did he talk about his business?" His tic jumped.

"No. We danced. That is all."

"Will you give a deposition to the court?"

"I cannot."

"Why?"

Mimosa reached into the pocket of her shorts and pulled out a badge. Her Cuban accent vanished. "I can't because you walked right into the middle of a sting operation. If I divulge anything about that night, our case is blown."

Her name was not Mimosa, but Sonia Tillotson, and she wasn't Cuban. The badge was Federal. Victor took a few minutes to come to grips with it all. The Feds ran in and out of Miami all the time. Ops here, ops there . . . ops normal. But this time their precious operation interfered with an innocent man's life. He couldn't come to grips with that, no matter how beautiful the ops leader was.

He realized she had left the room and he looked up in time to see her returning from the kitchen with two glasses of orange juice. "Mimosas?"

She smiled. "No, straight juice. Drink up, you'll need your strength."

"Ha, ha." He reached for one of the glasses. "Knock out drops?"

"No."

"What about those goons who mugged me last night?"

"What goons?"

He took a small sip. The cool liquid tasted like plain Minute Maid. "Don't hand me that. I followed you here. Parked down the street. Two men hustled me by the hat shop. Ruined the kidney I was gonna give my cousin one day."

"They weren't my men. Did you see them? Did they say anything?"

"Didn't see either of them. One said you weren't mine and told me to get lost — in no uncertain terms. Cuban accent."

Sonia picked up her cell phone and punched in a speed dial number. She said something in words he didn't understand, carried her part of a short conversation in the same language, hung up.

"What was that?" Victor asked.

"Swedish. Lessens the chance of our targets picking up something." She paced the floor with her orange juice in hand.

The Feds were paranoid as hell, but he would be, too, in their shoes, especially considering he had wondered about the safety of the juice. He should have listened to the logic, gone to see Armando Cruz, and stayed out of this mess. Now it was too late.

Sonia stopped her pacing, finished her orange juice in one long swig, looked at him over the top of her glass. In just that motion, she became Mimosa again and swayed toward him. "You are a handsome man. Virile and sexy. A generous mouth, not a mean one like some. How would you like to play my Latin lover, Victor?"

He reached for her and she fell into his arms, kissing him quickly, then pushing away. He wanted more and pulled her to him. He returned her kiss, long and hard, before releasing her. After all, Latin men made the best lovers, and he was the best of the best.

She walked to the wing chair across from him and sat straight. "For show only. We have a job to do."

"For show . . . for now. I've been told Cuban men are irresistible." He smiled lazily at her.

She wiggled back in the chair. "We'll see, Victor. We'll see. Now . . . about the men who beat you."

"Yes?"

"We think they are part of the group we're watching. If so, you're fortunate to be alive. I didn't know they watched me, too. We'll need to accelerate our plans."

"What group?"

"We've been at the Plaza Cubano for a few months. Your client showed up every Saturday night the entire time we've been there. I've danced with him each time. We checked him out and discovered a few peculiar circumstances in his background."

He frowned. "You checked him out because he danced with you?"

"That wasn't the only reason we checked him out. He also met with one of our targets on each of those nights."

"What kind of peculiar circumstances did you find?

Or is that an allowable question?"

"It's allowed." She smiled. "We checked you out, too. After you were so careful following me home last night, I wondered what you were up to."

"You knew?"

"Of course. You must be very proud of your brother."

"Yes. But how —"

"How is not important. The fact your brother is a SEAL is. It gives you more credibility."

"I assume that's important?"

"Of course it is. It gives us a higher degree of trust in you."

"And you're certain the man who tried to ram my kidney down my ass wasn't one of yours?"

"Absolutely."

Victor let this information sink in. "Let me get this straight. You were suspicious of Armando before Miami PD picked him up for his partner's murder. Correct?"

"Right. We're still interested."

He would come back to that. "Armando said he was with you at the time of the murder."

"Yes, he was. We were at the Plaza Cubano."

"Armando's attorney retained me to find you, get you to confirm his story, and have you to make a statement that would clear him. He didn't want his wife to know where he was, which I thought was dumb on his part, because it would all come out anyway." He paused for a few seconds, tapping his index finger against his lips.

"But it wasn't he didn't want his wife to find out," Victor went on, "it was he didn't want information about the Plaza Cubano to be made public."

"I'd say that's a good assumption."

"You said you're still interested in Armando."

"Yes. A Cuban group bent on causing terror and confusion down here had a new infusion of cash late last year.

We came down to investigate."

"An old group with a new direction. That means lots of local ties. They could be dangerous." He rubbed at his tic.

"They *are* dangerous. They have proven ties to al Qaeda."

"Cubans and al Qaeda? Cubanos are not Muslims."

"No, but they have the destruction of our country in common. Al Qaeda money was filtered back through an Iraqi oil company who used it to pay for equipment from Russia. The Russian company then sent the excess to the Cuban group, through its contact in Havana."

"You have proof?"

"Yes. Sealed affidavits, copies of shipping documents and invoices, bank transfers. We have it all." She nodded.

"Do these people know they're puppets?"

"No. They believe they are financed solely by the Cuban government. They don't realize al Qaeda would annihilate them, too, given the chance."

"How does Armando fit in?"

"We think he's the money man. His partner found out, and one of their thugs killed him. With Armando's complete knowledge and blessing. His partner had made contact with us."

"Armando's hoping you'll give him an alibi, and he can continue as before."

She smiled. "I knew you were smart. I saw it in those dark bedroom eyes the first time I met you."

Mimosa or Sonia — it didn't matter — she was one sexy woman. "I'll tell Armando you refused to give a statement. That you were afraid of your brothers. He's a Cubano — he'll believe it."

"He'll have to risk an indictment or expose someone else."

"Yes. I wonder which he'll choose."

Armando Cruz had requested a meeting on Monday morning and had been furious when Victor told him Mimosa refused to give a deposition. The guards had restrained him and removed him from the meeting room. Armando's attorney hadn't been pleased, either. Victor was glad he had been paid cash up front.

Victor did not see Mimosa again until the following Saturday night. He was at the bar of the Plaza Cubano when she arrived. A different red dress, but every bit as sexy as the first. He played with his drink until Mimosa found him at the bar.

"Hello, Victor. I am glad you have come tonight." She kissed his cheek, then rubbed at the lipstick mark with her thumb.

He smiled as she seated herself on the barstool next to him. "Would you like a drink?" he asked.

"Yes, thank you. That would be nice."

She traced a finger along his cheekbone, and he squirmed. Sonia had told him to come prepared, and he always carried his 9mm Beretta, but so far, this was more play than work.

He signaled the bartender. "Mimosa for the lady. Her usual."

The bartender nodded.

"I have missed you, Victor." She smiled her Mimosa smile and touched his sleeve.

Had he not been watching, he would have missed it, so light was her touch. The bartender brought the drink and orange sections. Victor paid, indicating he should keep the change.

They drank and made small talk for the next half hour, each observing what they could see of the room. Tonight was the night. Sonia had told him earlier Federal agents were stationed outside. Inside, too.

She leaned over and whispered in his ear, "At one A.M. there is to be a meeting in the back room. At one-ten we move."

Her voice rustled like fine silk. She bathed his earlobe for the benefit of any watchers. Victor shifted on the barstool and nodded. He moved his hand and caressed the top of her breast. Her skin was every bit as silky as her voice.

"That's nice, Victor. You play your role well. Unless I tell you differently between now and then, at one-oh-six, by the clock above the bar, I want you to ask the bandleader to play *Malaguena.* Right then. If he refuses, offer him this." She flashed the corner of a one hundred dollar bill and slipped it into his jacket pocket. If he still does not play it, get the crowd chanting *Malaguena.* Understand?"

Again, Victor nodded. His fingers strayed to the cleft between her breasts.

"Ah, Victor, you take your part seriously. That is good. *Malaguena* will be the key for things to begin. As soon as the music or chanting starts, I want you to guard the exit door to the right of the bandstand. See it?"

A dim red exit sign glowed above a black door. "Yes."

"Now . . . go to the men's room. Inside the folded bill is the photograph of a man. We prefer you let no one through that door. But by no means let the man in the photograph through."

Victor felt the weight of the small 9mm he kept strapped to his leg. "I'll be right back."

Locked in a stall, Victor unfolded the bill. His tic returned. The photograph was of Armando's attorney.

Victor returned to Mimosa and danced with her until

she excused herself. He looked at the clock — 1:06. While they danced, he had tried to pick out the agents inside. No one had looked like a Fed to him.

He walked to the bandstand and tapped the leader on the shoulder. "You know *Malaguena?"*

"Si, but this is the last song in this set."

"There's a hundred in it for you, if you play it now." He held the folded bill out between his index and middle fingers.

The bandleader shook his head then looked at the bill and wet his lips. Seconds ticked by, each longer than the one before. After what seemed like hours, the musician gave a curt nod and snatched the bill from Victor's fingers.

He signaled the band to stop. A groan went up from the dancers. Victor stepped to the edge of the bandstand.

The bandleader said, "Ladies and gentlemen . . . we have a request for an old favorite . . . *Malaguena."*

Applause went up, and the band broke into the familiar melody. Victor walked down the few steps and made his way through a clutch of mostly empty tables to stand beside the exit door. His palms had begun to sweat, and he wiped them on the front of his trousers.

He leaned against the wall and brought his right foot up to rest against the wall, too. His Beretta was within easy reach, and if the lawyer approached, he could come from only one direction.

The clock above the bar read 1:11. Mimosa was nowhere to be seen. Maybe something had gone wrong. No flack-jacketed Feds had burst through the front door. The band finished the song and left the stage. A guitarist brought out a stool, lowered the microphone, and began playing *Blue Spanish Eyes.* Mimosa's eyes flashed in Victor's mind.

Another glance at the clock — 1:17. Had Sonia set him up? It hadn't felt like that. He decided to wait until one-thirty. Twenty minutes was long enough.

No one approached him. No one ran toward the door. He searched the face of every man in the room. None resembled Armando's attorney.

From the corner of his eye he saw a flash of red. A quick look told him it was Mimosa. The clock read 1:28. She moved toward him as if she were a supreme lioness stalking her mate.

Her arms wound around his neck and she kissed him, her tongue ravaging his throat. She broke away and smiled. "Come with me, Victor, I want to show you something. Try to look like I'm taking you to the back for our mutual pleasure."

Victor took her offered hand and followed her. The look wouldn't be difficult. She led him past the bar, down the short hallway to the restrooms. At the end was a door. Mimosa opened it and led him inside. It was another short hallway, dim like the club. An armed FBI agent stood just inside, against the wall. Sonia pushed open double doors at the end.

They stepped into a room bright with several overhead lights. One end was like a warehouse with crates resting on metal shelving. The other end looked like a high-tech office, with two computers, printers, a fax, scanners, a copy machine. Several cell phones lay on the desk top.

Agents talked in soft voices to lessen the chance of being heard. Two teams swept for bugs.

In the center of the room, a large round table with a dozen or so chairs pulled out around it stood littered with cups. But that wasn't all. Six pipe bombs plus other explosive devices and walkie-talkies lay on the tabletop amid scattered papers, blueprints, and maps.

"This is it, Victor. We apprehended every single one of them. They were all here, and they didn't suspect a thing. Thank you for your help."

Another set of double doors opened to the back alley, where several vehicles were parked. Two men were handcuffed to a round metal handrail beside the door to the alley. A man with an ATF ball cap opened the back door of one of the cars and Victor saw a man handcuffed inside. He did not see Armando's attorney. "Where's the man in the photograph?"

"Over there." Sonia pointed toward the wall next to the doors back into the club. Victor turned. Yes, that was him. He lay on the floor surrounded by three men with big yellow FBI letters across their backs.

Sonia said, "He tried to make it out the door . . . must have slipped."

Victor's machismo acted up. He had been pumped—adrenaline still flowed. He wanted to be part of the hunt, part of the finale, the one to bag the assholes and take the glory. Instead, he couldn't get past the feeling he had been shuffled out of the way. "So . . . what part did I really play?"

She looked down at her feet then back up at him. "We put out the word you were the agent."

"What! You should have told me. I would have been prepared, acted differently."

She shook her head. "That's just it. You *would* have acted differently. These people knew you. They needed not to see a change. And as long as you were in full view, no one would harm you. The only risky time was when I sent you to the men's room, but I knew you could protect yourself." She touched his cheek and smiled.

"And *Maleguena?*"

"A diversion. We needed that, too. Since you've been back here, we've arrested the keyboard player and the bartender. Both had a warning buzzer to alert anyone in this room. We came in through the back."

His brother had talked about creating diversions. They were often necessary. And it wasn't every day a Miami PI participated in something of this magnitude. The role he played might save lives, maybe even his brother's. Victor's bruised ego stopped gnawing. "What's in those crates?"

Agents were taking them from the shelves and opening them to inspect the contents.

"Let's go see," Sonia said.

Victor swallowed hard when he saw the contents of the first box. Moon suits . . . full hazmat gear, not just gas masks. Several other unopened boxes had the same markings. Another crate contained automatic weapons. Another, more explosives, and another, detonators and ammunition. Those were just the ones he saw. Others remained stacked on more sets of shelves.

They walked out into the balmy night. Two men were offloading a forklift from a large flatbed truck. Others were busy on radios or guarding the vehicles holding prisoners.

"See you, Sonia," one agent called.

She waved.

They reached the street. Sonia said, "How about we walk on the beach?"

He took her hand and led her across the street. They went down the steps to the deserted white sand. Sonia stopped. She reached down and removed her shoes before they continued toward the water's edge. There was no moon, and as they moved away from the lights of Ocean Drive, stars popped out one by one over the dark water.

Sonia waded into surf above her ankles then tossed first one shoe, then the other, far out into the breaking waves. "I never want to see those suckers again. Goodbye, Mimosa."

She had a wicked left hook. He would remember.

"You know what, Victor?" she said, walking back to

him.

"What?"

"I love Miami. And I've always wanted to make love on the beach with a handsome man I liked." She ran her fingers down the front of his shirt, unbuttoned the top button, the next. Her fingers caressed his chest. She kissed the hollow at the base of his throat. "To hear the surf. Have it touch me, surround me."

Victor wrapped her in his arms and kissed her. She tasted of oranges. "Sonia?"

"Yes?"

"I wanted to make sure it's you, not Mimosa."

"It is us, Victor. Did you not always desire a threesome?" She laughed.

"This is Victor. Anything for you . . . and you." He kissed each eyelid.

Two palms grew near the surf's edge a few feet ahead. Perfect. No more diversions. Oh, yes . . . Victor loved Miami!

Bone Appétit

Andrew McAleer

PI Tony Valletta was invited to a time at a place in Boston's historic North End.

"Did you search his crotch?" The Old Gent asked his two-fisted goon, Paddy McDoherty.

Paddy nodded and held this out to offer:

"Yeah. I searched his knob, Boss. What there wuz of it."

"All right, watch the damn door."

"OK, Boss."

"Sit down, Valletta. We'll order steaks."

They settled into the far corner booth of the Old Gent's private steakhouse, Willow's Grill. Willow was the Old Gent's surname and he exhibited the depths of his creativity pool when naming the establishment.

"So . . . you couldn't keep your nose outta this thing, Tony? Had to go running around in high G."

"What thing?" Valletta said.

"What thing! You know what that answer is, Tony?"

"Tell me, Mr. Willow."

"It's: Blah! Blah! Blah! Freakin' blah! Freakin' blah! . . . Blah! Freakin' blah! That's what it is, Tony Valletta."

"You have a way with words, Mr. Willow."

"Uh-huh. What did you have to gain by budding into my dog track, Tony? I had Clocker Dan down at the track all set with the spreads. I'm asking, what is it that you want, Tony?"

"What do I want?"

"Uh-huh."

"What every PI wants. I want to believe in the soundness of the Euro dollar, Peter Pan, that hotdogs are made of real meat, that virtue is its own reward . . ."

With the palm of his left hand, the Old Gent began patting his stomach.

"Enough, enough, enough, Tony. Enough. A hundred years ago, Valletta, it was something to have a little beef around the middle. A little mound, you know. It was the sign you'd made it, that you were successful. Sometimes my belly feels a hundred years old. Well seasoned it is. I can't tell you all the things that have gone through here," he said, still patting his stomach.

"Try."

"Shut up! But it's seasoned. I'm seasoned. What'll you have, Tony?"

"The porterhouse."

"How?"

"Rare —"

"Good."

"— with a baked potato."

The Old Gent dipped his head a few times and then said, "I heard you were half Mick. You want some Irish freakin' root take your trade over to Southie with all the other smelly Mick flounder bellies. I call the Scotsman in all the way from Portland. I set it up with Clocker Dan so that the Scotsman has a fat day at the track. And what do you do. . . ? *You* take him over to the horses."

"I slipped. I knew I should've worn my Jack Purcell's

that day."

"You sure did slip, Tony. By the way, here you get pasta as a side dish. Cabbish?"

"Cabbage. . . ? Sure."

"Take it to Southie, Tony. Anyway, you know how the Scotsman likes to win at the track. I had everything neatly arranged with Clocker Dan. It was beautiful. And then you come along and peek under my pillow. You set me back, Tony. Way back."

A long smile flitted over Valletta's map. He slid from the leather booth and stood up to leave. Goon Paddy shuttled over and, with a 9mm automatic, persuaded Valletta to dismiss the notion.

The Old Gent head-beckoned and Paddy departed back to his post. Next the Old Gent came at his guest this way:

"Tony, come on. I figured at least half of you would have some respect."

Here a black arm with a white, linen cloth draped over it glided up and took dinner orders.

"I had an uncle who used to fetch deer," the Old Gent started, "and he'd toss the liver on the skillet. Bang! Twenty seconds one side. Bang! Twenty seconds on the other and it was done. Just like that. All over. Liver would jiggle and gurgle all over his tongue like old whore teats. I mention that because you ordered your steak rare. Do you like it that rare? Rare as my uncle?"

"No. Do you?"

"I like my liver that rare. Especially the liver of PIs who stick their bloody noses into my business."

Now the black arm came with two Absolut martinis; the green olives were the size of human eyeballs.

"Where were we?" the Old Gent asked.

"Cheers! Well, Old Bloke, you were talking about me bloody nose and me bloody liver," Tony Valletta said, before stepping into his Absolut.

Now the Old Gent's eyes were slits.

"Give me one damn reason why I don't have my man Paddy give you a lift home right now?"

"Well, we both like dogs."

"You have a dog?"

"I do."

"What kind?"

"Lab. Yellow. Only three legs." Tony Valletta wasn't kidding.

"So it's true?"

"'Tis."

"Don't go Irish on me, Tony. I was just starting to tolerate you. What's —"

"— Her. She's a she."

"Her name? What's her name?"

"Lady."

"It's an okay name, Tony, but I figure you have more color that that. Why'd you stick the bitch with that name? I think you could have done better."

"I picked her up used. She came with it so I figured why hassle the poor thing with a new name."

Presently the black arm stepped forward and delivered two rare porterhouses flanked with angel hair pasta and buttered okra.

"Used?"

Carving around the long, spearlike bone of the porterhouse, Valletta cut into the sirloin portion and gouts of blood popped into action.

"Yeah, used. Few years ago I was driving through some white socked community along Route Twenty and saw this place called Buddy Dog so I bounced in and looked around.

At first I just took Lady out for a walk you know . . ."

"Right to give her some fresh air. Go on."

"Right. I mean she's stuck in this little cage not much bigger than the little wine cages I passed on the way in here where all you and your rich patrons keep their highbrow stash of vino."

The Old Gent laughed as he patted his chops with a linen napkin.

Tony Valletta again: "Anyway, so that's it. I give her some fresh air and she's still with some kick left in her so I bundle her up and take her home."

The Old Gent was jousting flesh off the bone of porterhouse when he said, "That's a good thing, Tony. You did a good thing. You know the porterhouse collected its name from a cut developed in Porter Square right here in Cambridge?"

"Uh-huh."

Using his steak knife he pointed at Tony. "When I was a kid every so often a cow would escape from the stock-yards and book down Mass Ave into Harvard Square. The streetcars would get all piled up as the butchers chased the beast all over Harvard Yard. Imagine a cow in Harvard Yard today."

"Well . . . still has its share of jackasses."

"Hah! It's a good cut, the porterhouse. How'd your pooch lose her leg?"

"Guess she was hit by a car when she was a pup." Here the PI washed down some mignon cut with some more eighty proof. He continued. "Left her front right leg completely paralyzed. The ugly suck who owned her just left her leg dragging around so she was taken away and shipped to Buddy Dog."

Valletta sliced off a sprig of fat and then gazed at the blade of his steak knife.

"Like to use that thing wouldn't you, Tony? Paddy

wouldn't go for it."

Tony smiled. He was getting close to the bone now.

"I like you, Tony," the Old Gent said while lifting his napkin. "I wish you stayed out of this. Now things are messy with Portland. There's not much I can do. You're the one who chose to run with the hare and hunt with the hound." He made his napkin into a ball and tossed it on the table. "I think we're done here."

Valletta drained his martini. He lowered his glass and the queen olive stared back at him. One final hoist and the olive saw no more.

"No coffee?" Tony said.

"Coffee. No coffee here. Cappuccino. You want coffee go to freakin' Dunky Donut or whatever the heck it's called."

Tony elevated his shoulders and let them drop back into their pockets before he suggested:

"Cheesecake?"

The Old Gent tightened his lips and shook his head at his guest. The black arm delivered him a single cappuccino.

"Paddy will give you a lift."

"Straight home and put me to bed?"

"Something like that, Tony."

"Who'll take care of Lady?"

"Paddy will take care of her."

A pause hung heavy while steam lifted from the Old Gent's tiny cup.

Tony Valletta looked at his nearly empty plate, the naked j-bone of the porterhouse the only remains.

"Mind if I get a doggy bag? Lady likes bones."

For the black arm's amusement the Old Gent jerked his head in approval.

"Sure. Lady can have a bone, Tony. I had this uncle who used to give my dog chicken bones. All the time chicken bones. Everywhere he went the dog ate chicken bones. I'd say, 'Uncle, Angelo, don't give my dog chicken bones. It'll cut up her insides.' He kept doing it. He wouldn't listen. Then one day she died. Her gizzard all cut up and it was all on account of the chicken bones. Those things can kill you."

"And when you stuff a track pup with them before a race they don't stand a chance at placing anywhere at the head of the pack."

"It evens out the odds, Tony."

"Maybe."

Tony looked up and the black arm held a doggy bag containing the porterhouse bone.

After a long pause Tony Valletta retrieved the remains of what was to be his last meal. Blood was already sweating through the cheap bag decorated with a pattern of Roaring '20s newspaper headlines.

"Adios, Tony."

Tony was up on his feet by this point.

"You're going to kill Lady too, aren't you, Willow?"

"Paddy will give her your bone. She'll be gnawing away all happy. She won't know what hit her. Not like you. It wouldn't be smart for me to be running around with a three-legged yellow Lab, Tony. Remember my seasoned stomach. I didn't get this successful being a stupid head."

"You still have a way with words, Old Man."

"Clear off, Tony."

"So long, Old Man."

"Paddy, you sure you checked his trousers?"

"He's clean as boiled bone, Mr. Willow."

As Paddy led Tony to the exit Tony could hear the Old Gent ordering another cappuccino and a heavy slice of strawberry cheesecake.

Paddy and Tony walked down a dimly lit corridor of the restaurant. The entire time Paddy's hand enveloped

Tony's left shoulder.

The wall to their left consisted of wine cages where frequent patrons corralled their special blends of wine.

Gleaming brass plates held the inscriptions of the wine bearer.

As they passed the Old Gent's wine locker the image of Lady leaped into Tony's mind.

Tony Valletta gripped the end of his doggy bag, spun, and buried the spear of the porterhouse bone into Paddy's stomach. It went in like a meat thermometer into a raw, fat roast beef.

One swift move and Paddy McDoherty was relieved of his 9mm. Another swift move and the PI smashed the back of Paddy's head, sending him into a bloody heap.

Tony unsheathed the bone from Paddy's gut, shucked off the bag's redundant headlines, and walked back into the main floor of the restaurant.

It would have been just as easy for Tony Valletta to fill the Old Gent's stomach with Paddy's 9mm, but he knew Lady.

The old girl loved a juicy, meaty bone and would enjoy the additional seasoning.

Who Put the Armadillo in the Avocado Dip?

Linda Summers Posey

"Stacy, he's here." Francine Brownlee, fund-raising chair for the Alliance of Animal Advocates, fanned herself with a lace handkerchief. "Finally."

"Who?" I joined her at a window inside the private dining room at La Casita de River Oaks, Houston's most upscale Mexican restaurant.

"Walt Walters. That's his black BMW pulling into the valet parking area. You know, Waterbeds by Walt." She dragged me toward the entrance, boot heels clicking on the tile floor.

"As in, 'My wolfhound, Winnie, sleeps like a baby on a Waterbed by . . . ' that Walt?" Every Houstonian knew Walt Walters from his loud and folksy late-night TV commercials.

"He just joined the Alliance, and he promised me a big donation." Francine smoothed her sleek black hair and inspected her makeup in an ornately framed mirror hanging near the door. "He's going through a messy divorce, poor thing. But I want him to forget his troubles tonight.

That check of his will put my fund-raiser over the top, so you must help me make him feel welcome."

"My job is to make him feel secure. That's why you hired Matt Martin Investigations." If I didn't blow this guard duty gig, my boss might trust me with a real PI assignment next time. I wasn't expecting any trouble at Francine's benefit, but I shifted into my best apprentice private eye mode anyway and scanned the room for hazards to her illustrious guest.

The banquet room teemed with preening animal lovers of every stripe, all decked out in "Texas casual" wear. After stuffing themselves at the buffet for the first twenty minutes of the event, they'd stampeded the dessert table. "I don't think anybody will bother your guest," I said. Except maybe Francine, a forty-something divorcée whose dangling diamond earrings were the only thing pedigreed about her.

"Ah — I should hope not." Francine fought off her Texas Hill Country drawl. "Is there still plenty of food? Walt's a big eater."

How did she know Walt's eating habits, I wondered. Maybe she'd already put a move on the mattress mogul. "Last time I looked, all the dishes were full. Fajitas, veggie tacos for the vegetarians, chips, and a huge bowl of guacamole."

Francine checked her designer denim jacket. A small green stain marred one lapel. Obviously, she'd sampled the avocado dip, though I hadn't seen her stop to eat all evening. "Oh, dear, just when Ah need to look mah best." The drawl was winning. She scrubbed at the spot with her handkerchief.

"You look fine," I assured her. "I can barely see the stain." For this I'd given up a night of classic movies from Blockbuster? The things PIs do to keep their customers feeling "secure."

"Now, smile. Ah — I'll introduce you to Walt, then I'm going to show him off to Libby Crane. She might have beaten me for president of this organization," Francine added with a note of disdain, "but *she's* never brought in a heavy-hitter like Walt."

A deep male voice rumbled from the entrance. "Howdy, Francine. Sorry I'm late." Houston's waterbed impresario, unmistakable in his trademark string tie and cowboy hat, charged into the room at an impressive speed, given his bulk. He pumped Francine's outstretched hand far longer than necessary while he rambled on about the pressures of business and traffic.

"So good of you to come." She planted a lipstick-laden kiss on his cheek and grinned like a canary-sated cat. "I'd like you to meet Stacy McReady. She's handling our security tonight."

"Pleased to meet ya, Miz McReady. Now if you ladies'll stand back, I'm gonna grab me some chow." Walt headed for the buffet, took a plate and started piling on the food. "I'm so hungry I could eat a grizzly bear. Not that I would, o' course, not at an Alliance get-together," he added. "I'd be in deep trouble if I ate —"

"But, Walt, darlin', I want you to meet some of our members." Francine sidled between him and the table.

He sidestepped her. "Can't chew the fat on an empty stomach. What's this? Guacamole!" He grabbed a chip, scooped up a generous glob and popped it into his mouth. "Dee-licious."

"I'm so glad you approve," she cooed, eyelashes batting like hummingbird wings. "You'll have to try my homemade sometime. Now I know you want to meet Libby Crane."

Walt suddenly couldn't find his mouth with his taco. "Libby Crane?" His voice squeaked like a rusty gate. The color climbing his neck told me he and Libby were already acquainted.

"Certainly. She's our president," Francine said through gritted teeth.

Without turning around, he jerked his head toward the bar. "I'm kinda thirsty, Francine. You reckon that bartender has any Lone Star?"

She fought off a wrinkle-inducing frown. "I can find out. Stacy, would you?"

"And while Stacy's getting me a beer, Francine, would you see if you can snag me one of them desserts? Pecan pie, if they have some."

With a huff Francine trotted away to do her star's bidding.

He leaned toward me and whispered, "If you're the security here, you'd better guard me from those two women."

"You didn't know they were both active in the Alliance?"

"I just met Libby last week. I had no idea she was president of this outfit."

I stifled a grin and dashed off in search of Walt's favorite brew.

The bartender turned up his nose at the idea of Lone Star in La Casita, but a little flirting with a waiter produced the desired results. I presented the longneck to Walt, and he drained it in a single gulp. He still had his back to the room, as if that would save him from a confrontation with his lady friends.

I took the opportunity to grab a fajita, savoring the tang of marinated beef and grilled onions, the soft warmth of the flour tortilla. The free food was part of my payment. The Walt Walters side show was a fringe benefit.

A flock of Alliance members soon surrounded him, eager to see and be seen with their famous new donor. Walt buried himself in the crowd, shaking hands, answering questions about Winnie's welfare. But his restless gaze darted around as if he were an animal cornered by one too many predators.

By the time Francine rounded up a slice of pecan pie and lured Libby Crane away from her gaggle of girlfriends, Walt's admirers had trailed off to the tables. He worked his way back to the buffet for another fajita. He actually seemed to have shrunk a few inches. Trying to make himself invisible, I guessed.

But Francine waltzed Libby right up to him and made the introduction, sounding smooth as melted margarine — and just as synthetic.

The fringe on her western shirt fluttering, the Alliance president enveloped us in a cloud of White Diamonds and leaned over to kiss the air beside Walt's cheek. Spotting the red lip print on his jaw, she glared waspishly at Francine.

"Walter," Libby gushed, dragging him back to the buffet, "it's so good to see you again, sugar. Now I haven't had a moment to eat. Tell me what's good."

Speechless for once, he followed her along the table while she filled her plate. "I'll just taste everything," she said, "except the avocado dip — I'm allergic."

Francine fumed until I thought she'd explode. Finally, she slipped between them and pawed Walt's arm. "Whenever you're finished eating," she murmured, "I hope you'll say a few words to our crowd."

With a subtle elbow nudge, Libby flanked her rival. "Yes, Walter, I'll introduce you as our newest corporate supporter."

Francine planted her boots in a stance that would have made Rocky Balboa proud. "Libby, he's my guest. I'll introduce him." Her voice rose a notch. "Walt, *darlin'*, I'm so thrilled you're taking a stand for the protection of endangered species."

I was afraid Walt Walters was about to become an

endangered species himself.

"Mmmph," he mumbled around a bite of taco and concentrated on digging into the dip.

His chip snapped in two.

"Gosh darn it, this guacamole's playin' hard to get." Frowning, Walt set his plate down, picked out a large flat chip and eased it into the dip as if he were panning for gold.

Crunch.

"My Gawd! That's a hell of an excuse for a garnish."

"What is?" Francine crooned in a tone sweet enough to calm a crazed pit bull.

Grabbing a serving spoon, Walt excavated the guacamole in earnest. The spoon clinked. He froze. "It's a goll-darn armadillo."

Libby's eyebrows rose halfway to her frosted hairline. "Don't be silly. Can you imagine an armadillo in La Casita de River Oaks?"

"Don't have to. The blamed thing's right here."

I stared over Walt's shoulder. Sure enough, a leathery brown oval poked from the surface of the dip, two pointy ears at one end, skinny tail at the other. The creature didn't look like a plastic toy — it looked quite real and quite dead.

Their feud forgotten for the moment, Libby and Francine crowded around to see what Walt was talking about. Libby turned a lovely shade of avocado green. Francine waved her handkerchief over the bowl like a magician trying to make the animal vanish.

I was pretty sure disposing of dead armadillos wasn't in my boss's orders for tonight, but I didn't have much choice. I had to salvage the fund-raiser, not to mention my PI career.

I took the spoon from Walt and scraped dip off the shell. Albert didn't move. *Albert Armadillo?* I almost had to laugh to keep from crying. So who'd tossed poor Albert into the dip? And why?

The cute little thing was just a baby, no bigger than a taco, not counting the tail and ears. No wonder the armadillo had become an unofficial state mascot. "At least it's not road kill. The shell's intact," I said. "I'll take care of it."

Walt latched onto my shoulder. "I wouldn't toss that if I were you. It's evidence."

"And we wouldn't want anyone eating the evidence, would we?" I signaled a waitress to cart the remains to the kitchen. Eyeing the bowl as if it were full of raw sewage, she shook her head and darted out a side door.

In a moment the restaurant manager, Kate Longoria, strode in with the trembling waitress in tow. Kate resembled an older Jennifer Lopez except for her ivory-pale skin. At the moment I attributed her coloring more to shock than to great skin care or Anglo ancestors.

"I can't imagine how that animal got into my guacamole," she said. She swore not even a gnat could have landed in the serving dish without her knowledge. Then she spoke to the waitress in Spanish. I couldn't understand a word, but I was glad I wasn't on the receiving end of that blast. The girl hung her head and whisked the bowl away, Kate at her heels.

Walt watched all this with a grim expression. "I want to see my doctor," he said. "The heck with him — I want to see my lawyer."

Perspiration glistening on her upper lip, Francine yanked his elbow and drawled, "Why don't Ah go find you another drink?"

"Beer? On top of armadillo-infested guacamole?" He clutched at his throat.

With a smile as phony as a paint-by-numbers Mona Lisa, she stroked his arm. "Ah know how devastated you feel, Walt. Libby, what's the Alliance going to do about this awful accident?"

"The Alliance?" Libby sputtered. "I'm sure the restaurant is responsible. And *you* booked the restaurant."

While the two women squared off, rumors of disaster spread through the room. The crowd's buzzing rose from lazy-bumblebee to enraged-hornet volume.

Libby wheeled around in a swirl of red fringe and announced, "There's nothing to worry about. Please, continue enjoying your dessert." When the uproar settled to a low hum, she turned on Francine. "If this incident ruins my benefit —"

"*Your* benefit?" Francine cried. "I'm the one who pulled everything together."

"Ladies, ladies." I raised both hands. "This won't solve anything."

"Darn tootin'," Walt put in. But when the three of us faced him, he muttered, "I'll just mosey on out of here. I have a lawyer to call."

"Oh, no, please don't leave," Francine said.

"Not over this unfortunate accident," Libby added.

Walt snorted. "Accident's hind toe. I can't afford to back an organization that exposes its members to leprosy."

"Leprosy?" Francine and Libby chorused. Libby glanced over her shoulder to see if the other members had heard, and Francine brandished her hanky like a battle flag.

"You bet. Armadillos carry leprosy." He hightailed it toward the door.

I waylaid him and steered him back to the dining room. "No one leaves."

"Why the hell not?" he asked.

"I don't believe for one minute that armadillo dropped in on its own. They're shy creatures. They stick to the underbrush unless they get trapped in your headlights."

"Sure," he said, "you can spot 'em along the bayou anytime. Who knows how it got in here? But if anybody gets sick, there'll be some serious charges."

"At least malicious mischief," I agreed. "Or reckless

endangerment. Not to mention cruelty to animals. I have to find out who did this. That's why no one leaves," I added as the two women caught up with us.

"Anything you say, Stacy," Libby said. "I have every confidence in you."

Francine scowled at her, then at me. "That *is* what I hired you for."

"Did you notice anyone lurking around the table?" I asked her.

She spread her hands helplessly. "I was far too busy."

"'Course she was," Walt said. "I bet everybody in the room came to the table sometime."

"So I'll interview them all." I didn't mention that my fee would go up with the overtime.

"But they're my guests," Libby protested.

"*Your* guests?" Francine cried. "Why I —"

"I don't care whose guests they are," I said. "I'm going to interview them. The staff, too. The Alliance has plenty of enemies — furriers, animal researchers —"

"You're forgetting the rodeo," Libby interrupted proudly. "Last year my committee picketed the livestock show for promoting the carnivorous lifestyle."

"That's my point," I said. "Any one of those groups could have a spy here."

"And you expect me to cool my heels while you question everybody in kingdom come?" Walt said. "Not a chance."

"No, I expect you to be a good guest and help keep everyone else calm."

"Well," Francine meowed, "you should start your interviews with Kate Longoria. I've heard she owns a fur coat."

As in, crime of the century, I thought. "That doesn't mean she'd sabotage an Alliance party. She could lose her job." I ignored Francine's protest and headed for the kitchen.

The food preparation area could have adorned a health department poster. Stainless steel counters and appliances sparkled. Even the trash cans looked spotless.

Before I could ask Kate if she made the guacamole herself, she strong-armed me and toured me around the room. One by one her squadron of cooks and waiters stood at attention, while Kate made like a drill sergeant presenting her troops for inspection. Her underlings smiled on cue, but when she turned away, more than one shot a rattlesnake-fang glance at her back.

Maybe someone had planted Albert to get Kate's goat. Maybe they'd all conspired against their overbearing boss. Shades of *Murder on the Orient Express.* The thought of someone killing an animal — even a lowly armadillo — to spite a human being — even a spiteful one like Kate — made me sick.

But by the time I'd interviewed the staff, my conspiracy theory had gone the way of the passenger pigeon. Though every employee I questioned seemed relieved to be out from under Kate's eagle eye for a few minutes, getting back at their boss was hardly a motive. I was convinced they'd all rather die than lose their jobs — or touch an armadillo.

I couldn't find any evidence of tampering by outsiders either. No one had noticed anything out of the ordinary. No strangers had wandered through, no unexpected deliveries had arrived.

That left the Alliance leaders and their guests. Walt seemed to know an awful lot about armadillos, but a brand new supporter of the organization wouldn't have any reason to sabotage a fund-raising event, would he?

My money was on the leaders. Francine and Libby had made no bones about their stinging rivalry for Walt, the big donor they were both trying to impress — or seduce. Was either of them that desperate to make the other look bad in front of him? They'd sure seemed eager to lay the blame for Albert's appearance at each other's feet. Francine had that tell-tale green stain on her jacket. And Libby refused to eat the guacamole claiming she was "allergic." But where would either of these social butterflies find an armadillo, dead or alive? I'd sort out motive and opportunity after I confronted them.

I found Francine and Libby near the buffet table, talking in harsh whispers.

"You have no business pursuing Walt," Libby said, "not when he's so vulnerable."

"What, Ah'm supposed to stand aside while you reel him in?" Francine replied. "And what do you mean by vulnerable?"

"You haven't heard? That shrew of a wife is taking him to the cleaners. She'll own Waterbeds by Walt before the year's out."

"Well, Ah know for a fact he's keeping his mansion on the huge wooded lot overlooking Buffalo Bayou."

No wonder Walt made that comment about seeing armadillos along the bayou. My theory of motive and opportunity shifted. I cleared my throat. "And just where is your guest of honor?"

Libby and Francine jumped, stared at me, then at each other. Libby had the grace to blush. "He went to the restroom."

"He told *me* he needed to check with his answering service and his cell phone battery was dead," Francine said.

"Why?"

"I think he's your man."

Before Francine could work up a glow of triumph, I added, "I mean *our* man. He couldn't get his stories straight to you two just now, and he's already tried to leave the scene once. I bet he's flown the coop again. Now quick, help me find him."

Francine scoured the kitchen, while Libby braved the men's room. I headed for the front door just in time to swipe his car keys from the valet. When Walt sneaked around the corner of the building and into the covered drive, I nabbed him and hauled him back inside.

Francine and Libby raced up to join us. "How did you know?" Francine asked.

"The first clue was the fact that he knew about armadillos carrying leprosy and lurking along the bayous. Not exactly the kind of information most people have at their fingertips."

"What does that prove?" he countered.

"Not much," I admitted, "unless you had motive, means, and opportunity. Francine was saying you have a wooded lot on the bayou. The perfect place to find a family of armadillos. So you had the means. And we left you alone at the buffet for several minutes, plenty of time to bury the armadillo in the dip. Plus you're the only person who's bolted — twice."

"To think how I fantasized about that house," Francine blurted. She clapped a hand over her mouth and shook her head.

Libby's lip trembled, but she darted a sympathetic look in Francine's direction. Then she pulled herself together and turned to me. "You covered means and opportunity. What about Walter's motive?"

"You said it. His wife is soaking him in the divorce. I bet he can't afford to pay his gas bill, much less his pledge to the Alliance."

"That's horse hockey." Walt looked pleadingly from Francine to Libby to me. "I love my wolfhound Winnie and all God's other critters."

I couldn't resist rolling my eyes. "His ad campaign — his whole reputation — is based on how much he loves animals. If he backed out on the Alliance, he'd look bad in front of the organization, his customers, the entire community. He needed a darn good excuse for refusing to ante up. A man with motives like that wouldn't think twice about dumping poor little Albert in the guacamole."

"Albert?" the two women chorused. "Awww."

I gave a sheepish shrug, and for the first time since I'd met them, Francine Brownlee and Libby Crane really smiled — at each other. Then the smiles faded, and they turned on Walt Walters in unison. I thought seriously about turning him over to them for justice.

There's Something About Julie

Dorothy Rellas

I'd lived for thirty years believing my mother was right, I had the Irish "gift." A sixth sense for judging people. I went along with it — until a poker game in a Boston hotel five years ago. Good group of guys, out for a friendly game, right? Wrong. I lost the bar I owned, my car, and my wife. It occurred to me my mother hadn't known what the hell she was talking about. Like everyone else, I didn't know who was on the level and who was trying to con me. A few people you read easy. Others sail right under the radar. Like Julie. Although when Nick Gamble's call woke me up Thursday morning, I hadn't figured that out yet.

"You alone, Al?"

"Yeah."

"There's a major problem," he said, a tremor in his voice. "Come over to Gamble's right away."

I looked at the clock next to my bed. "Geez, Nick, it's four-thirty, still dark out."

"I'm at the restaurant — lookin' at a warm body."

The line went dead. "A warm body" could mean anything — a stiff or some broad he'd brought back from wherever he'd spent the last three days. Which didn't make much sense, considering I'd had to run out of Julie's apartment at one o'clock that morning, carrying my clothes and dressing in the stairwell when Nick had come back unexpectedly from his three-day trip.

I threw on the same clothes I'd worn at Julie's and was on the Santa Monica Freeway ten minutes later.

Traffic was light at five o'clock, but I kept the speed down. Never rush into what could be a setup. I'd done that more than once before.

After the poker game when I'd called on a full house and lost to a royal flush, a bogus one I discovered later, I'd drifted to L.A. and gone back to doing PI work. Found a job with an old veteran and earned my California license. When my boss decided to retire, I took over the agency. I'd worked for three, four dozen clients, not all of them interested in sticking to the truth.

Too many times lately, I'd teetered on the edge of losing my license. Once I almost ended up in jail. I'd been left with shit on my face often enough to know I didn't have it. No Irish 'gift.' How was I going to make it as a PI? Maybe I was better off owning a bar. The job wasn't any easier, but I'd be dealing with a better class of people, even if a lot of them were drunk most of the time. I decided to keep handling cases while I moonlighted to get the down-payment. Six months ago, I started as a bartender at Nick Gamble's Restaurant.

It was a great place to work — with a few wrinkles — like the sharpies who came in a couple of times a week. They wore Armani suits, diamond rings on their pinkies, smoked fat cigars, and congregated in Nick's office. I finally put the puzzle together.

They were mob types, guaranteed. Flew into LAX from Las Vegas with cash skimmed from casinos aimed for offshore bank accounts.

Then Nick hired Julie to sing and play the piano. Five nights a week she sat at a Steinway grand on a raised stage behind me, that low, whispery voice making me itchier than hell. I was still thinking of Julie a half-hour later when I arrived at Gamble's. Nick looked up when I walked in. I stationed myself behind the bar.

"Al, sit over here." He nodded to the stool next to him.

"Bartenders don't function too good on the other side of the bar, Nick," I said. "Makes 'em nervous."

Nick sat hunched over, nursing a drink, fidgeting with the glass. There was no hint of his usual flamboyance. I knew right then — 'warm body' hadn't referred to a broad.

"Al, we're in big trouble," he said. "I just came back to town and stopped in for a drink. I thought I heard voices coming from the employees' lounge, so I went in." He looked over at the curtains in front of the hallway that led to the lounge and his office. "Julie was inside."

My eyes opened wider. Damn. Nick had found out I'd been sleeping with his girlfriend. A big wave of panic crept up my spine while I poured myself a double. "What happened?" I asked him, playing Mr. Cool.

"She's dead, Al. Sitting in a big chair back there, staring at TV, a bullet in her forehead."

My hand lurched, and my drink splashed on the counter. Julie? I'd just seen her a couple of hours ago. My legs felt like two soggy straws, but I managed to walk out from behind the bar and sit down a few stools away from Nick.

"You shot her?"

"You crazy? I loved her."

I stared at the stage behind the bar, seeing Julie at the piano, feeling a heavy weight in my chest.

"Strom's gonna have a field day with this," Nick said.

The name snapped me out of my funk, and the memory of Strom's visit a few nights ago floated to the top.

"Strom came in right after closing on Tuesday," I said. "Looking for you. I told him you were out of town, didn't know when you'd be back."

Nick's face turned a chalky white. "He knew I'd be gone."

"Didn't seem to." I clutched the glass with both hands. Strom had sat about where Nick was now. He'd eyed me with undisguised contempt, spread his fat hands flat on the counter and half stood up, as though he was getting ready to spring over the bar-top and push me up against the back wall. Then he'd grabbed my tie and yanked me toward him. With his other hand, he'd reached inside his jacket, pulled out a gun and glared at me long enough for my life to flash through my mind.

After he'd given me a little tap on the head with the end of the gun, he slid off the bar stool. His two goons had come forward from a back table where they'd been sitting.

"Tell Nick I want to see him, pronto," he'd said. Then, like handlers rushing the champ out of the ring, the three had walked across the dance floor and disappeared into the shadows.

I told Nick what Strom had said.

Nick took a couple of short gasps. "I need help, Al. I wanna hire you to find out who killed Julie."

His eyes were bloodshot, and the frown lines between his eyes were etched deep. From Julie's death or worry over Phil Strom? I wasn't sure. All I knew was that no way could Nick Gamble have killed anyone. If I'd read him right. Of course, that was the problem, wasn't it?

We both heard the sound of footsteps and looked toward the back hall.

"Better get hold of your lawyer." I slipped off the stool. "How long ago'd you call the cops?"

"I'll do it now," Nick said.

"Call the cops about what?"

Lou Marino stood in the doorway, white apron on and curly blond hair under a small white cap. He'd drifted in from Vegas about two weeks after Julie had shown up. He convinced Nick that with his ten years' experience in the kitchens of some of the big Las Vegas casinos, he'd turn Gamble's Restaurant into a culinary dream. Nick, who loved food almost as much as he loved women, fell for it. I had to admit, there'd been a definite improvement in the restaurant's cuisine. The tomato sauce stopped tasting like watered ketchup, and he actually made ravioli from scratch.

So why didn't I like him — aside from the fact that at thirty something he was a good ten years younger than me, good looking and a big hit with women. It was more than that. A feeling. A sixth sense that told me Lou Marino wasn't on the level.

Nick explained what had happened, and Lou's face clouded up.

"You're kidding. That cute little chick?"

"I'm gonna look in the lounge," I said, desperate to get away from Lou's gaze. It always cut through me like an Arctic wind.

Julie sat propped up in a chair, staring in the direction of the TV. She wore a short yellow dress with long sleeves and a pair of well-worn slippers. Small, barely five feet, with red hair, pale skin and freckles, she looked off-key with the big smear in the middle of her forehead. I felt like taking her in my arms and telling her everything would be okay.

I finally looked away and gave the room a quick inventory. No gun. I also didn't see the purse she usually had hanging from her shoulder or a jacket to keep out the night chill. Whatever had happened at Julie's apartment, she'd left in a hurry.

When I walked out of the lounge, I heard Lou back in his kitchen, giving orders to a couple of the crew that had just come in. Nick still sat at the bar, staring at the piano.

"Make the calls?"

He nodded.

A few minutes later, two detectives and a couple of uniformed cops arrived.

"Sgt. Bannon," one of them announced and jotted down our names and who we were in a small notebook. "So, what happened?"

Nick told him about finding Julie. While Bannon and his partner left to look at the body, I took Nick aside. "Don't say anything until your lawyer gets here."

Bannon came back and nodded to a table. The three of us sat.

"What time did you get here?" Bannon asked Nick.

Nick shrugged. "Musta been about five-thirty."

I glanced at my watch and frowned. It was six now, which meant that I'd taken Nick's call, gotten dressed and driven twenty-five miles from my Los Feliz apartment almost to the airport in fifteen minutes.

"Kind of early, wasn't it?"

"Just got back from a little trip. Been away since Tuesday — wanted to check the receipts."

"Where was the trip to?"

"I was on a boat aimed for Cabo. The weather wasn't too good in the south of Mexico, so we turned around and came back early."

"The deceased, Julie Savoy? She a friend?"

"Sang and played the piano here."

"Local?"

"Moved out from Chicago a couple months ago."

"I'll need the woman's address — and the people with you on the boat — who were they?"

Nick came up with some names, two couples who

were unfamiliar.

"Just the five of you?"

"Plus the crew," Nick said. He shifted on the chair and then flashed his disarming smile. "And a woman friend who's married. I'd like to keep her out of it." He looked embarrassed and pasted an aren't-I-a-bad-boy look on his face.

"We have to talk to her, Mr. Gamble, but we'll be discreet."

"I'd appreciate that," Nick said, the edge in his voice announcing that he had friends in high places who could take care of Bannon's future.

"I'll need phone numbers and addresses for all of them," Bannon said. "Especially, Ms. Savoy's."

Nick frowned. "I'll have to do some digging."

Bannon turned to me. "Al O'Rourke. Good old Spanish name."

He laughed, and I joined in, even though after thirty-five years, how many times had I heard the same joke in one variety or another?

"So, Al, you're a bartender here?"

I nodded. It was first name with me, I noticed.

"And what brought you out at five-thirty in the morning?"

"I called him when the boat docked," Nick answered before I said anything. "I wanted to know what had been going on while I was gone. You know, what kind of business we'd done, that kind of stuff."

My warning to Nick to keep his mouth shut had been like telling fish not to swim. I suppose reminding him that if he insisted on talking, he'd better stick to the truth would have been just as useless.

"You from around here?" Bannon asked me.

"Boston. Been here a few years."

Bannon closed his notebook. "That does it for the time

being, Mr. Gamble. Could you find those addresses now?"

Bannon followed us into Nick's office. "I'll check out some singers, Nick," I told him. "I'll be in touch if I find out anything."

"Don't go too far," Bannon called out when I turned and headed for the front door.

Where the hell would I go?

I melded into the early morning traffic, remembering the last thing I'd heard before closing Nick's office door. "I'm a really big fan, Mr. Gamble," Bannon had said.

Not surprising. Nick had been a jazz singer twenty years ago, made the transition to pop and became famous. Pretty good voice, great style, and a reputation as a ball breaker. There were whispers about Nick and the Mafia. No proof, but the suggestions draped him in mystery. Women fell all over him. He slept with more Hollywood stars than Sinatra's Rat Pack combined. Then a new style of music came in and Nick's career and sex life collapsed. He'd made a bundle, so there was no worry there. Just needed a place to line up women. And do his Las Vegas friends a favor. A couple of years ago, he'd opened Gamble's out near LAX.

A half-hour later, I was in Julie's apartment in Westwood. The first time I'd come to see her, I'd wondered how a singer in a bar could afford a two bedroom, three bath in a building where rents started at twenty-five hundred a month.

I'd noticed also that Julie hadn't accumulated much. Which meant it was a snap going through the living room and kitchen. The first thing I saw when I started on her bedroom was her purse on the dresser. I took out a checkbook, stuck it in my pocket and went through her billfold. A half-dozen business cards were stuffed in the section with the paper money. I put them in my pocket, too.

In case Nick hadn't picked up my signals about where

I was headed, I worked fast, aiming for the short hallway that led to the back exit I'd used that morning when Nick had unexpectedly shown up. I figured a half-hour, max, and the cops would arrive.

Time was running out so I almost skipped the bookcase filled with CDs. But it was close to the back hallway, so I took a chance. A savings passbook was stuffed between two CDs, and behind them, a plastic bag with a syringe inside. At the same time, I heard a fast rap at the front door and a key turn in the lock. I was downstairs and in my car within a minute.

When I parked in the restaurant's lot again, I went through Julie's business cards. They were all from Chicago. A TV repair shop, a couple of dress boutiques, and one from Jolie's with the name Sam written at the bottom with another telephone number next to it.

Ten thousand dollars had opened her checking account two months ago. The stubs showed two, three dozen checks — rent, groceries, Saks, a lot for cash. On the same day she'd opened her checking account, she'd opened a savings account with another ten thousand. Eight deposits had been made, ten thousand each, weekly since she'd been working at Gamble's. No hint as to who'd supplied them.

She didn't sing that good. A sugar daddy? Maybe, but not Nick. He wasn't crazy. Not even over Julie who could slip into your heart and start you dreaming about a future.

I'd hardly noticed her when she'd come into the bar the first night, except she'd looked like a kid.

After she'd gone to the back hall and climbed the few steps to the stage, I heard her drag the piano bench to the right spot in front of the piano, play a few chords, switch the mike on and off. The bar filled up.

Nick came in at nine and sat at his usual spot in the middle of the bar. I slid a Jack Daniel's on the rocks over to him. He raised the glass in a salute to the girl at the piano. Then the stage lights went on and it became real quiet. Or as quiet as it ever gets in a bar that's full of people more interested in booze than entertainment.

She played some nice progressions on the intro, a few imaginative patterns through an old standard then segued into another one. I'd played piano in a jazz combo when I was still living in Boston, so I knew how it went. The audience gave her five minutes. When they figured she was nothing special, the hush gave way to the usual murmur and clinking of glasses.

Then she started singing. At the first few chords of *Sophisticated Lady,* everyone quieted down again. They'd give her another chance.

Her voice was husky, low and unspectacular, and she had trouble sustaining some of the notes, but she knew how to end a phrase in the breathy way that keeps everyone from hearing just how much has gone out of a voice over the years. Nick would appreciate that. She had something else, though, a rare quality you didn't hear often. She directed the words to each listener as though the two of them were alone in the dim room. She was singing from the heart. Lady Day, the voice gone but with a vulnerability that brought back every disappointment and heartache. We'd all been the sophisticated lady: "Smoking, drinking, never thinking of tomorrow . . ." It was very quiet in Gamble's. She sang the last measures, "And when nobody is nigh — you cry." The note faded, leaving the air heavy with memories.

Everyone clapped and whistled. Even the younger ones who probably had never heard the song before, cheered. I was still thinking of that first night when I saw Bannon and his partner leave the restaurant. I took out my cell phone and called Dan, a guy I'd worked with in Boston who'd moved to Vegas and opened an agency. I told him to find out all he could about Julie Savoy in Chicago and Phil Strom in Vegas.

I walked into Nick's office without knocking. He was at his desk, talking on the phone. A guilty look flashed across his face when he saw me, and he clicked his cell phone off.

"What do you know about Julie?" I asked him.

He raised his eyebrows. "Not much. She's from Chicago. Had a little trouble with drugs — was in rehab just before she came out here. Swore she was clean."

"You giving her any money? Something extra every week since she's been here?"

He shook his head and clenched his mouth tight.

"Any of your mob friends come from Chicago?"

A brief look of panic flared in his eyes, and he tapped his fingers on top of his desk. "I don't know."

"Think maybe Julie was working for Strom?"

"Why'd he hire Julie? He didn't even know her."

I stood, then turned at the door.

"Maybe he wanted to send a message. When he came in the other night, he didn't sound like one of your biggest fans."

"I know these guys, Al. Trust me."

"Maybe Julie was working for someone who wanted to keep an eye on you — see if you were maybe skimming from the skimmers." I threw it out because it had occurred to me more than once.

"What the hell you talking about?"

"You find that out, you sure would be pissed. Might decide to take care of Julie yourself."

Nick was out of his chair and across the room before I'd turned the knob. He was a wispy little guy, shorter than me and about twenty-five pounds lighter, but when he poked his finger in my chest, he shoved me into the door behind me.

"I didn't kill her," he said, breathing hard, his face a mottled red.

I was almost sure he was telling the truth. Almost.

He stepped back, and I opened the door and walked out.

"And come in tonight," he hollered after me. "We'll be open."

I hadn't had a chance to ask him why he'd lied about the time he'd called me Thursday morning.

That afternoon, a half-dozen cops showed up at my apartment.

"Search warrant," one of them said and waved a piece of paper in front of me. "Just routine. Need to look around. And Bannon wants to see you, ASAP. With your car."

At the station they took my car to search and sent me to a room inside. Bannon let me sit for a few minutes and then walked in.

"Sorry, Al, but I need to ask a few more questions." He was holding his notebook.

"Any problems with the law back in Boston?"

"You already know the answer — no problems."

He read from his notebook. "You own a detective agency in L.A. now, started working for Mr. Gamble six months ago."

I told him about my plans to open a restaurant, and he wrote it down. "Try to remember what time it was when Mr. Gamble called you Thursday morning and when you arrived at the restaurant."

"I don't pay much attention to time. Especially when someone wakes me up. Early's all I remember."

"Found your fingerprints in Ms. Savoy's apartment. Visit her often?"

I'd worn gloves when I'd searched her place. Kind of stupid to forget about my earlier 'visit,' as Bannon put it. I could feel the handcuffs. "I was with her this morning.

Someone buzzed from downstairs. She pushed me out fast."

"What time was that?"

I shrugged. "Midnight, one, maybe. Like I said, I don't pay much attention to time."

"Who was her visitor?"

"She didn't say."

"What's your guess?"

"Don't have one."

"She was killed sometime between eleven last night and three this morning, not in her apartment, not at the restaurant."

He let a couple of minutes go by before he spoke again.

"Where'd you go after you left her place?"

"Home, to bed. And no one saw me."

"Own a gun, Al?"

"Yeah — with a permit. Keep it in my apartment in a desk drawer. Your guys should be finding it right about now."

He stared down at the notebook. "I heard you really had a thing going with Ms. Savoy."

"I liked her."

"You know your friend Nick Gamble liked her, too? Someone saw him going into her apartment at midnight Thursday."

"He didn't kill Julie."

"No? How do you know that?"

How did I explain to him about intuition and feelings and my Irish 'gift'? Which really didn't work most of the time.

"I just know." I was tired of the bullshit. "Sergeant, should I call an attorney? Or can I go now? I'm working tonight, and it takes me awhile to get ready."

Bannon got up. "You can go. No attorney necessary — yet."

When I walked into Gamble's, Cara the reservation clerk, told me Nick wasn't coming in. I walked into the nearly empty dining room, found a seat and ordered.

In a few minutes, Lou Marino himself brought me my whole dinner at once — lasagna, garlic bread, and a big green salad with mozzarella shaved thin on top. "How about a nice wine to go with it?"

I shook my head. "Off the booze right now," I said.

He sat down opposite me. "Nick told me you're a PI, looking into Julie's murder."

"Just poking around — lasagna's great, by the way. How long you been cooking?"

"A few years."

"In Vegas, right?"

"Mostly. In Boston when I started out."

"Which was when?"

"Hey, I hardly knew Julie. Not my type. So forget the questions. I have a kitchen to run." He started to slide out of the booth.

I speared a piece of lettuce. "Great salad. You ever work in Chicago?"

"Maybe once or twice." He stayed where he was.

"You ever meet Julie before she showed up here?"

"Never saw her before."

He was good at playing the role. I'd noticed that before, had all the nuances. When he was telling the truth, he relaxed. When he was lying, his smile kind of froze and his eyes were even deader and more zombielike. Very subtle changes, but I saw them — almost sensed the tension.

I was halfway through my dinner when my PI friend called from Las Vegas.

"Phil Strom works for one of the top boys here," he told me. "Haven't found a record yet. Julie Savoy had a string of arrests in Chicago, all for possession. Last time she was arrested, someone bailed her out."

"Who?"

"A law firm that represents the big mob family there. A Chicago cop I know said she was offered a deal if she'd name the guy who'd supplied her. She turned them down. The next day, the charge was dropped. I'm sending you all the reports."

"Check on a chef who works at Gamble's — Lou Marino. He started here right after Julie did. From Las Vegas, Boston before that. See if they know him in Chicago. And, Dan, have your friend try this number." I gave him the number printed on the business card I'd found in Julie's billfold. "Guy's name is Sam."

I sat in the booth, drinking coffee, thinking about Julie again. Sgt. Bannon hadn't been too far off. I'd liked Julie, a lot. Not that she ever came on to me — nor to Nick, either, that I'd noticed. She wasn't the type. She reacted to what people did to her. Just let things happen. I'd made my move, she responded.

Nick had been shocked over my accusations about the cash coming in from Las Vegas and that he'd helped himself to some of it. I figured I was right on both counts. But killing Julie? I couldn't figure the motive. I even had a hard time thinking Phil Strom was guilty. Just as likely it was someone I didn't even know, a dealer right here in L.A. or an acquaintance, a hard-luck junkie like her.

The next day, I was at the bar by late afternoon. Carla was at the reservation desk, and she looked worried.

"The place is falling apart, Al. Mr. Gamble still isn't coming in, and Lou Marino just quit."

Perfect timing. I went into Nick's office and opened the file cabinet where the employee records were kept. Julie's last reference was Jolie's Restaurant in Chicago.

Marino's application showed a string of Las Vegas casinos where he'd worked, mostly as a kitchen worker.

Some of the dates were missing and others didn't jibe. I wondered if Nick had even checked on him. Lou had said he started in Boston, but he was born in Chicago. And the culinary school he'd attended was there, too.

I was riffling through some other files when the door flew open.

"They've arrested Mr. Gamble," Carla said, on the brink of tears. "His attorney called and said you should keep the restaurant going until things are straightened out."

I called Dan in Las Vegas.

"Just hung up from my cop friend in Chicago," he said. "Lou Marino lives in a posh condo overlooking Lake Michigan. Drives a Jag, kids go to an exclusive private school and his wife does charity work."

"On a chef's salary?"

"Travels a lot," Dan went on. "Gives cooking demonstrations, also organizes parties, seminars for the same Chicago law firm that bailed Julie Savoy out of jail. They represent some of the top guns in the Chicago mob. Marino uses cash a lot, so it's hard to trace his income. With all his traveling, the cops've pegged him as an enforcer."

"You have the names of any of the places he's worked?"

Dan started reading. He'd reached the tenth name when I stopped him. "That last one. Jolie's?"

"Yeah. My friend said it was one of the best restaurants in the Midwest. Great food, owned by Sam Deluga. Very connected, if you know what I mean."

I knew what he meant, and everything started slipping into place.

"I'll call when I've run down the phone number," Dan said.

By two-thirty, the restaurant was empty. I turned the lights off in the bar area. Carla told me that Lou had left, but he was coming back after closing to leave his key and gather up his things. What did a chef have to gather up? Recipes? Favorite pots and pans?

I went into the kitchen. It was a big room, with deep fry vats in the island area, stainless steel ovens and cooktops along one wall and refrigerated units along the other. Every bit of space was used, and even quiet and empty, there was a certain amount of disorder.

I started at one end of the room and checked everything. Moved every pot, every frying pan, every baking dish. I went through cupboards and drawers. And found nothing. Not even a recipe. Inside one of the refrigerators, I felt around in back, stuck my hand in a bowl and came out with something that looked like flour. I tasted it. Flour. I was thinking it was a funny place to keep it when a noise made me turn around.

Lou stood there. "You lose something?" he said and very nonchalantly picked up two knives from a knife holder on the counter.

I dug into the bowl again and felt something familiar buried in the bottom. I wrapped my fingers around it.

"You came out here to take care of Julie, right? Kinda cozied up to her, maybe even fell for her. Why should you be different? But when DeLuga told you he was tired of giving her hush money every week, it was time to get moving."

He looked at me with that dead-eyed gaze that turned my blood cold.

"Turn around," he said.

"You started watching her place," I went on, ignoring his order. "When you saw Nick go in and me come out Thursday, you figured you'd get rid of Julie and set-up Nick for her murder at the same time. Talk about falling into it."

"With that imagination, ever thought of writing a book?" Lou raised one hand and a knife sailed past my head. It hit the stainless steel cabinet and clattered to the floor.

I swallowed and went on, still half turned, still with my hand in the bowl. "After Nick left, you went up and convinced her to go to Gamble's. What'd you do, tell her you had some pure stuff?"

He moved so fast, I didn't see it coming. Another knife. Only this one hit my left arm before it clunked to the floor. I'll tell you, it stung like he'd used an ax. But he was out of knives. I yanked the bowl out of the refrigerator along with a couple of the bowls and jars in front of it. Everything crashed to the floor, but I held onto the baggie I'd felt in the flour, with the gun inside. I managed to get it out at the same time Lou lunged. When I pulled the trigger, Lou fell, his head making a clanging sound when he hit the stainless steel cabinet on his way down.

Nick was sitting at the bar when I came in at five o'clock the next day. He was on the phone with an agency about a chef. My arm was in a sling, and it hurt like hell. I managed to mix myself a drink.

"I knew some of the Deluga family," Nick said, when I sat next to him. "Why would one of 'em put out a contract on Julie?"

"She and Sam Deluga had a thing going, and she found out about the drug operation he was running from his restaurant. She agreed to keep her mouth shut, but he could see paying her forever. So he sent Lou Marino out here to take care of her."

"And that shit found the gun in my desk and used it to kill her."

I nodded. "And hid it in the refrigerator. Nice touch."

Nick leaned forward. "I owe you one, Al. Although I was kinda disappointed you thought I was passing money for the mob in Vegas and stealing from them."

"I was goading you, Nick. Trying to get information, that's all. And how come you told Bannon you'd called me from the boat? At first, I thought you were trying to set me up."

He looked embarrassed. "After the boat docked early, I went to see Julie and we had a fight. I drove back out to the beach, just sat, looking at the water before I came here."

He took out his phone again. "Now I gotta find a chef and a new singer."

"As soon as you do, better find a new bartender, too."

"Hey, what happened to saving enough money to buy a bar?"

"Nailing Lou Marino, my confidence came back. Guess my mother was right, after all."

He frowned. "What does your mother have to do with it?"

"It's a long story. For now, I've decided to stay in the PI business."

He looked at the piano on the stage behind the bar. "I really thought Julie and I had something special. Even though I thought she might be sneaking around, seeing someone else."

My hand lurched, just like the night Nick had called me in and told me about Julie.

"A lot of guys wanted to get next to her, Nick," I said. "You know, there was something about Julie."

Raiding the Pantry

Kenneth Thornton Samuels

"Okay, there were two of them. White. Male. Late teens to early twenties. Dressed casually. Both wearing ball caps. One had large, horn-rimmed glasses. The other had a large Band-Aid over his nose. Can you tell me anything else, Mr. Hanrahan?"

Timothy Hanrahan, still called "Timmy" despite the fact that he was past sixty and looked it, thought a moment before answering. "Nah, except for them old baseball shirts they was wearing when they come in. With them caps, I thought they might've been coming in from some late night game, but the cops said they found the shirts and caps on the street just a block or so from here."

The tall, gray-haired man with the slight foreign accent and the Polish name that Timmy'd already forgotten, nodded. "Throwaways. They wear something distinctive that you'll be sure to remember, then discard it when they're a safe distance away. Makes it hard for the police to get a useful description. The glasses and the Band-Aid were most likely worn for the same reason."

"Really," Hanrahan said. That was more than the two cops from the Oak Park Police, the kid in uniform that took the report, and the other kid in civilian clothes that called himself a detective, had bothered to tell him. Just filled out some forms then left. This here cop, though, who wasn't much more than a kid himself despite all the gray hair, was asking a lot more questions, skillfully coaxing out details Timmy hadn't even realized he remembered. And he wasn't even a real cop. Just a guy sent out by the alarm company.

Cop or not, there was no denying he was an impressive guy. Tall, slim, with the kind of ramrod straight posture Timmy associated with the "lifer" non-coms he'd known in the service. And like those professional soldiers, this guy made a point of doing things with precision, from the way he wore his navy-blue suit, to the words he chose when he asked questions, to the way he pronounced those words.

Timmy looked over at the sign by the main entryway. THIS FAMILY BUSINESS IS OWNED BY FRANCHISEE TIMOTHY PATRICK HANRAHAN. Timmy always felt a swell of pride whenever he read that. He'd bought the store almost ten years earlier. After thirty years of working for other people, he was his own boss! Not the other night, though. He was taking orders from them two punks who come in waving guns around. Ten years without a robbery till then.

"Mr. Hanrahan, after the robbery we sent some technicians to check your alarm system. They said it was in perfect order. Why didn't you set it off?"

"I wasn't nowheres near the alarm button when they pulled the guns. See, like I told you, when they first come in I thought they was customers. They walk right over to the beverage case and act like they're looking for something. One of 'em looks up and asks do I carry Lakeshore Lemon Sparkle. I tell 'im sure and he says can you come here and show me. So I get out from behind the counter and walk over to the beverage case and out come the guns. I'm never close to the button during the whole show. After they leave, I figure hitting the alarm's like locking the barn door, so I just get on the phone and call 911."

The alarm company guy nodded, clicked his pen closed, put it away, thanked Timmy for his time, and left.

Max Donner, CEO and Board Chairman of The Kitchin Pantree, Inc., the fastest-growing chain of convenience stores in the Midwest (or at least Chicagoland), shook hands with the tall, lean man who'd entered his private office. Ramrod straight, wearing a crisply pressed, blue business suit, his tie knotted with almost military precision, but that shock of gray, almost white, hair was what first caught Donner's eye. Didn't seem to match the face. Kind of like that tough-guy movie star from the '50s, whatever his name was. Young and vigorous looking, but prematurely gray to add an air of *gravitas.*

"Nice to meet you, Mr. Pucinski. Or do you prefer Earl?"

"It's Errol," he answered, smiling to show no offense had been taken. His voice had more than a trace of Eastern Europe in it, but with an overlay of Chicago's South Side.

"Like Flynn?"

"Exactly. My mother's favorite movie is *Captain Blood.*"

"I was just thinking that you looked a little like a movie star. The guy who played Cochise in *Broken Arrow.*"

"Jeff Chandler. I've been told that before, but aside from the hair, I can't see the resemblance."

Donner looked more closely at the business card his visitor had handed him on entering. A line drawing, in blue ink, of a man in cowboy garb holding a shotgun while standing guard in front of a stagecoach. In black ink, the words "Wilson/Farragut Security Services." Three of the four corners listed information like the type of services offered ("Armed, Uniformed Guards; Alarm Service & Response; Armored Cars; Criminal, Civil & Industrial Investigations; Polygraph Examinations; Insurance Adjustors"); the address of the local office; and the e-mail, phone, and fax numbers. In the lower right hand corner was the name "Errol Pucinski" and the title "Senior Investigator."

"What can I do for you, Mr. Pucinski?"

"I'm here about a series of robberies taking place in Kitchin Pantree stores throughout the area."

"A series? Random hold-ups are common in the convenience store business, unfortunately. That's why we include an alarm service in our franchise package. But I've heard nothing about a series."

"We've concluded that at least four robberies of Kitchin Pantree stores have been committed by the same people. That's why I've come to see you today."

Pucinski went over to the wall and indicated a map of Chicago and the surrounding area on which all of the Kitchin Pantree franchises were indicated by colored pins.

"The first one was at this store in Buffalo Grove three weeks ago. The second was four days later in Winnetka. The third in Lincolnwood ten days after that. The most recent was two nights ago in Oak Park. What common elements do these four stores have?"

"All of them are in the immediate Chicago area, but none of them are in Chicago itself."

"Precisely. What else?"

"Each one is in a different town."

"Very good. That's why the robberies haven't been connected before now. Each was a fairly typical late night robbery of a convenience store, which are, as you correctly point out, one of the most frequent targets of such crimes. To the police force in each city concerned it would be an isolated incident. If the robberies had occurred in Chicago, even in different districts, a connection would probably be made sooner. As it is, if it weren't for the fact that all your franchisees have alarm systems installed by Wilson/Farragut, the robberies might not've been linked."

"Even so, I'm not sure where you come into this. Do you want the Corporate Office to hire you?"

"You've already hired us, Mr. Donner. Or rather, your franchisees have. You made a Wilson/Farragut alarm system one of the selling points to potential franchise buyers. That alarm system didn't do any of those store owners any good. It should have. When a business is under Wilson/Farragut protection, we take the obligation seriously."

"Then what do you need from me?"

"I need to find out what else these stores have in common. The four stores are owned by people who have no common traits. They're not all the same ethnic group, or age group. They bought their stores at different times, for different reasons. Nevertheless, although there are a hundred and twenty-seven Kitchin Pantrees in the 'burbs, thirty-three between Buffalo Grove and Oak Park, those four were singled out. So they must have something in common."

"What do you think that is?"

"I have no idea, and that's why I'm here. The answer might be in your corporate records. Maybe the same corporate representative sold them their franchises. Maybe they were financed by the same bank. Find the connection and I'll be a long way towards finding the robbers."

Anybody who knew the exact number of Kitchin Pantree franchises in suburban Chicagoland was bound to favorably impress the man who'd started the business. Moreover, Donner, like Pucinski, felt an obligation to his franchisees. The alarm system had been made part of the package precisely because so many potential owners were nervous about hold-ups. If they were getting victimized despite state-of-the-art crime-fighting technology, then Donner owed it to them not to impede old-fashioned detective work. A few phone calls to the right people in the right offices, and Pucinski had a clear path to the information he needed.

"What if the common link isn't in our files?" asked Donner.

"Then I'll have to go back to square one and re-interview each of the victims."

Not every Kitchin Pantree store was open all night, but this one, in the south suburb of Harvey, was. The two men who entered, young, wiry, athletic, dressed in ball caps and worn baseball shirts over nondescript jeans and T-shirts, walked in at about one A.M. Except for the tall, slim, gray-haired proprietor behind the counter, they were the only people in the store.

The first guy, who had a Band-Aid prominently displayed over his nose, looked at the counterman and gave him no thought at all.

The second, who wore large, old-fashioned horn-rimmed glasses, looked a little closer at the storekeeper, and decided he looked tougher than most people he'd seen working the graveyard shift at convenience stores. Best get it over with quickly.

Horn-Rims walked over to the beverage case, and began looking for something, without apparent success. He looked up at the storekeeper and said, "You got any of that new stuff, Mister, that Lakeshore Lemon Sparkle."

"You bet I do," the gray-haired guy answered. He had a slight foreign accent. "I keep all our Lakeshore Lemon Sparkle here behind the counter, right next to our robbery alarm button. Which, by the way, I've just pressed."

The gray-haired guy reached under the counter, and came up holding a Remington, pump-action, twelve-gauge shotgun. He racked a round into the chamber and said, "The police'll be here shortly to take you into custody. Meantime, you're under citizen's arrest. Both of you put up your hands."

Band-Aid, who'd said nothing to this point, found himself too shocked to say anything now. Horn-Rims managed to stammer something about just what they were supposed to have done.

"Oh, I suppose the concealed handguns you're both carrying will do for a start. Since you didn't actually get around to sticking me up, I don't suppose they'll be able to charge you with robbery, but the police in Buffalo Grove, Winnetka, Lincolnwood, and Oak Park will undoubtedly want to talk to you about the stores you robbed in those cities. You'll be warned about your right to remain silent and all that. My advice is simply to come clean. There's no reason for you to take the rap yourselves. It was all Anderson's idea, wasn't it? He cased all the jobs when he made his deliveries. Why should he get away?"

Thoroughly abashed, they raised their hands.

"So the common element was that all four stores used the same beverage delivery service?"

Ralph Conway, commander, at least for tonight, of Harvey PD's midnight watch, was speaking to the tall, lean, gray-haired security officer who was seated across from Conway's desk.

"That's right. I might not have noticed the connection if one of the owners hadn't mentioned the particular soft drink the offenders asked for. When I checked the corporate records, I found that the victim stores all used the same beverage delivery service. When I checked further, I found out that they were all serviced by the same deliveryman, William Anderson. He was casing jobs for his accomplices while performing his regular work duties with Cook County Beverage Supply. Once I made the connection, I re-interviewed every victim and confirmed that they'd each been asked for help finding the same soft drink, Lakeshore Lemon Sparkle. Since the robbers appeared to be moving in a southerly direction, I simply staked out the first store on Anderson's route south of the most recent robbery. When they hit, I was ready."

"That stakeout shouldn't have been handled alone."

"I wasn't really alone. I'd notified both the local beat officer and our own alarm response unit of my presence. They both arrived at the store within a minute of my activating the alarm."

"What was the point of that lemonade drink?"

"He pushed it on each potential victim knowing it to be a slow seller. Each store only carried a small quantity. Consequently no store owner would think it odd that anyone looking for it would need help. It moved slowly enough that Anderson could be reasonably certain that it wouldn't be sold out by the time his accomplices arrived to perform the actual robbery, which meant that each store owner would have to step from behind the counter to help what each thought to be a legitimate customer."

Conway nodded. "Hell of a job, Pucinski. *Hell* of a job. Shouldn't be any problem getting a warrant on this Anderson character. And with the statements his accomplices are making, his conviction should be dead-bang. This'll make your agency look damned good."

"And, after all," Pucinski replied, "making Wilson/Farragut look good is really what it's all about."

Holiday Bonus

Nick Andreychuk

"Sometimes I really hate this job," Earl Stack muttered to the empty washroom, as he replaced the lid on the toilet tank.

Checking the toilet had been a last ditch idea, so he left the stall feeling irritated. On his way out of the warehouse's men's room, he grabbed the cart of cleaning supplies from where it propped the door open. He grumbled to himself all the way down the hall and into the mop room, where he deposited the cart, pulled out his cellphone and called his client — A.K.A. his boss in his current undercover position. "This case is a bust," he said in greeting.

"Hello to you, too," Jonathon Dumont said from the comfort of his home. "Look, I don't care how long it takes you, you're not leaving there until you find my money!"

"I'm telling you the place is clean." Literally. Stack's own home had never received as much cleaning attention. Dumont had made it crystal clear that he didn't want anyone second-guessing Stack's janitorial status, so he'd had to play the part to a T. Dumont had even gone so far as to tell Stack not to wear a fedora, as if only private investigators wore stylishly comfortable hats. In compliance, Stack had opted for an old mesh baseball cap while he'd mopped the floors and searched high and low for stashed loot.

"Look," Dumont said. "I wouldn't have hired you if I didn't have good reason to suspect that the guys at the loading bays were fudging the inventory records and selling off goods under the table."

"They must've snuck the cash out already."

"We've been over this. I overheard one of the guys tell another guy that he'd split up the cash and they'd have it on Friday — *tomorrow.* And tomorrow's the last workday before the holidays. My Christmas bonus is going to be low this year because of those thieves. Thanks to their scamming, my division's not as profitable as it should have been, and therefore my percentage bonus will reflect that."

"So what kind of percentage do janitors get?"

"Very funny. Only upper management gets a monetary bonus. You — like the rest of the employees — will be getting a nice big turkey . . . *if* you don't blow your cover and you come back to work tomorrow night."

"Some bonus. I can see why those guys, with all that back-breaking labor, would be tempted to increase their take-home pay."

"Hey! Those turkeys aren't cheap, and we're giving out ones that are already cleaned and stuffed. Besides, those guys are still breaking the law."

"Yeah, well, I don't see you calling the cops."

"And you'd better not either. I need that cash now. I'm not waiting for it to go through all of head-office's bureaucracy before it's worked into my division's profit-loss statements, and a tiny bit of it *eventually* trickles down to me by bonus time next year."

As they talked, Stack wandered through the large, box-filled warehouse to the cafeteria in search of a place to sit. He sank into an orange vinyl chair, and rested his legs on the adjacent seat. He barely listened to Dumont. Where hadn't he looked? His eyes fell on the kitchen. He'd checked all the cupboards, tins, and cans, but . . .

"Everyone's getting their bonuses tomorrow, right?" Stack asked, cutting off something Dumont was saying about firing the loaders.

"What? Right. So what?"

Stack stood and weaved his way through the tables to the swinging kitchen door. "Stuffing," Stack said as he pushed open the door. "I have a hunch some of the turkeys have *green* stuffing." He entered the walk-in freezer, after propping its door open with a stepladder. "Damn, it's cold in here."

"What an astute observation. Now, what about them turkeys?"

"There're a lot of 'em, but they all have stickers with names on 'em. Whose should I check first?"

"Try Smitty's — if his has bread crumbs, then they all do."

"Okay. Let's see. Sikes. Slavan. Yep, they're alphabetical. And here's a bird for Mr. Stanley Smith." Stack turned the turkey around on the shelf. "Hmm. There's definitely some regular stuffing in here, but let's see if that's *all* there is." He pulled a small folding knife from his pocket, and sliced open the cellophane. He jabbed the knife into the frozen stuffing and . . . pulled. A small chunk came out a little too easily.

Stack grinned. *"Bonus."*

"Is it there?" Dumont sounded as excited as a dog in a hydrant factory.

"Unless the grocery's offering some weird instant rebate on their turkeys, I'd say that I've found your kickbacks."

"Clever, clever bastards. If they'd have gotten caught, they'd just claim they thought the cash was part of their holiday bonus. Okay, here's what you're going to do. Check all the turkeys. Take the cash out, replace it with some *pink* memo paper from the supply room — that ought to send a loud-and-clear message — and make a list of all the thieves."

Stack rolled his eyes at the phone. *Should I add your name to the list?* "Is that all, boss?"

"Yes, and make sure to reseal the turkeys. Then bring me my money!"

Stack ended the call without further comment. More than a hundred turkeys awaited his inspection.

He carted the stuffed birds to the warm kitchen in small batches, and placed them on the counter next to an industrial-sized roll of all-purpose food film. As he went through them, he ignored the names on the turkeys with regular stuffing, and confirmed that a bird had his name on it. He loved hot turkey sandwiches.

Stack waved goodbye to the night watchman on his way out of the building. Fortunately, the security guard, a retired cop with a bum leg, rarely left his seat at the front desk. Still, Stack could understand why Dumont hadn't tried to find and remove the loot himself. It would have been awkward trying to explain the contents of the garbage bag slung over his shoulder.

Stack breathed easier once outside. Being close to dawn, there was only one car besides his own in the parking lot. He hurried towards it, striding carefully on the icy asphalt.

Just as he was about to open the driver-side door, a woman jumped up from in front of his car.

"Hi!" she yelled, startling Stack and causing him to slip. He fell flat on his behind and lost his grip on the bag.

A young woman with hot-pink lipstick smiled at Stack as she reached down to help him up. Embarrassed and annoyed, he shooed her hand away. "Sorry," she said, as she reached for the bag instead. "I didn't mean to scare you."

Stack scowled. "You didn't scare me, but I wasn't expecting someone to jump out at me in the middle of the night in an empty parking lot."

"Sorry," she repeated. "Hey, so like can you give me a lift?"

Stack looked her up and down and realized she was holding his bag. Just as he was about to snatch it back, she turned and walked to the passenger side door. "I don't live very far and I like need to get home before my parents murder me, okay? Please? Pretty please?" She'd adopted a puppy dog expression which Stack couldn't help but grin at.

"All right. Get in."

"Thanks," she said as she wriggled herself into the seat. "Hey, what's in here?" she asked. She pulled at the ends of the garbage bag.

Stack reached across the seat and grabbed the bag before she could get a good look at its contents. "Nothing," he said. He stuffed the bag under his seat, sat down, and closed the door on the chill air.

"My name's Candice Dumont, by the way, but everyone calls me Candie, so call me Candie okay, because I hate it when people call me Candice, like my parents, even though I keep telling them that it's Candie, not Candice."

Stack felt out of breath just listening to her. "Wait, are you related to Jon Dumont?" he interrupted.

Her eyes lit up. "Hey, do you know him? Yeah, I guess you do 'cuz I just saw you come out of his work. Duh — how stupid can I be? Yeah, he's my lame-o dad, oh, but you're not going to tell him that I said that right 'cuz you know, he's not so bad."

"Actually," Stack interrupted again, "it just so happens that I'm on my way to pay your papa a visit."

Candie's eyes lit up. "Really? How come?"

"Oh, uh, just work stuff. But never mind that. What are you doing out at this time of night?"

"Okay, I was like at this party, and it got late and now I have to get home and get ready for school before like my parents notice I'm not home, and —"

"I get the point."

Candie smelled of pot, but what did he care? She wasn't his daughter. Besides, her eyes were focused, so maybe the smell came from her teased-out hair.

Stack started the car and defrosted the windshield.

As the air in the car warmed up, Candie opened her winter jacket. Stack noticed that her body had matured quicker than her verbal skills.

Soon they were on their way.

"Hey, I just realized you never told me your name. And, like, are you gonna tell me what's in the bag?"

"It's Earl Stack and I told you before, it's nothing. Just something I picked up for your papa."

"Oh pooh — it's probably just some boring paperwork. And you're just some boring old janitor."

Stack had nothing against janitors, but being a private eye carried a gritty coolness to it that many women found exciting. And though he had no intentions of laying a hand on the jailbait sitting next to him, he nonetheless couldn't resist the urge to impress her. "Actually," he said, "I'm a private eye."

"Ooh, that sounds *dangerous,* are you like investigating a murder? No! I bet you're like undercover to spy on the workers to see if anyone suspects that my dad had Sanders whacked."

"Who's Sanders?"

"Okay, he's like this guy who —"

"Forget I asked. Your dad didn't kill anyone — at least not that I know of — and there haven't been any murders at the warehouse."

"Oh, oh, I bet someone's stealing from the company."

Stack imagined Candie in a classroom, squirming in her seat, waving her raised hand at the teacher. For some reason, he pictured her in a short-skirted, midriff-baring cheerleader's uniform.

"A-ha, so I'm right," Candie said, taking Stack's silence as affirmation. "So do you like carry a gun? Oh, and, and have you killed anyone? With your bare hands? Do you know a lot of gangsters?"

And on it went — a constant stream of questions, with barely any room for Stack to say "yes" or "no" or "none of your sweet-assed business."

Because of — or in spite of — Candie's constant yammering, time passed quickly. Stack drove into a residential area with large, two-story brick homes that were more imposing than impressive. The outside lights were on at Dumont's house, making it easy to read the number by the two-car garage.

"Okay, so I'm gonna sneak around back," Candie said as they pulled in the driveway. "I'll be able to like get up to my room while you distract my father. Puh-lease don't tell him, okay?"

"No skin off my back," Stack said. He turned off the ignition, reached under the seat for the garbage bag, and stepped carefully out of the car, mindful of more black ice.

Candie slipped out of the car and around the house before Stack reached the front door.

Dumont answered the door and invited Stack inside.

Stack stepped in far enough to close the door, but didn't remove his shoes or enter further into the warm house. "Here's your dirty money," he said as he shoved the bag at Dumont.

Dumont grabbed it greedily, and looked inside. "Thank you for your services," he said. "Your check will be in the mail."

"It'd better be, or else I'll have a few choice words with —"

"— the police?" The female voice came from behind Dumont.

Stack's mouth dropped open.

Dumont spun around. "Who are you?"

The woman Stack knew as Candie — looking older with her hair pulled back and her lips wiped clean — flashed her badge in response.

Dumont's face paled considerably. "How . . . how . . . how'd you know?"

"We caught some guys selling merchandise out the back of a truck. They didn't reveal their source, but the boxes originated from your warehouse. You have a lot of explaining to do." She smirked at Stack. He fully expected her to say, "Fooled you, didn't I? Some private eye you are." Instead, she said, "You're free to go, Mr. Stack."

Stack tipped his hat to her, shrugged his shoulders at Dumont, and called it a night.

The next evening, Earl Stack went to work at the warehouse as scheduled, but he left an official note of resignation on Jonathon Dumont's desk. The pile of phone messages and unopened mail indicated that the manager hadn't been in that day.

Stack had a strong feeling he wouldn't be paid for his PI services anytime soon. At least he'd get paid for his janitorial services — including his nice big turkey with special green stuffing.

Crow's Avenue

Robert Lopresti

"You're dependable, Marty," said Alice. "That's what I like about you."

Within a mile of us there were a dozen people who would have disagreed with her judgment. Some would have been happy to put their opinion in a notarized statement, signed in blood if necessary. But they weren't in the car, so they didn't get a vote.

"I try," I said modestly.

"Unlike *some* people," Alice continued. "There are *some people* you can't depend on at all."

That was a reference to Colin, her fiancé — "ex-fiancé," she declared now — who had brought her down from Toronto for a long weekend. When Colin discovered that one of the casinos was hosting a big exhibit of baseball memorabilia, with some legendary all-stars on hand, he had disappeared. Alice was responding with the legendary grace of a woman scorned.

"I never want to see that little swine again," she said. "I never — My, there are a lot of casinos on this road, aren't there?"

I nodded. "Pacific Avenue is the main drag in Atlantic

City. Half of the casinos are here."

Alice frowned. She was pretty in a pale, English way. About five years younger than me, in her late twenties. "That's the *Atlantic* ocean south of us, isn't it? I left Canada, but I didn't change *coasts.*"

"Right. Atlantic Avenue is one street north of us. I don't know what genius named this one Pacific."

"Atlantic, Pacific, Boardwalk . . . These streets are all on the Monopoly board, aren't they?"

"Right again," I told her. "The game was invented a few blocks from here."

"All those little green houses," she mused, and then laughed. "I suppose I could buy a real one now, couldn't I?"

She could make an impressive down payment, that was for sure. That's why I was driving her around.

Tom Juarez, the head of security at Rose Casino, had called me an hour before. I had just finished dinner and was settling down with the racing page to try to figure out why the horses I bet on all seemed to suffer mid-race crises.

"Marty, we have a poster child. Can you come over?" I hadn't been thrilled about trudging out into the furnace-like evening, but a paying customer is always right.

"That Mr. Juarez is so nice," Alice was saying. "You'd think the casino would be *mad* that I won so much money. But he hired you to protect me, and gave me a free room —"

"Casinos don't mind big winners," I explained. "Unless they cheat, of course. Casinos live on the odds. And if the odds are a million to one against somebody having a lucky streak like yours, and a million people pass through your floor every year —"

"Then someone is going to win," said Alice. "I see."

"Did they take your picture?"

"Yes. At the craps table."

I nodded. "Next time they do a full page ad your smiling face will be there. The text will say 'Alice D. of Toronto won umpteen thousand at the Rose Casino.' A lot of people will see the ad and say 'if she can, so can I.'" That was why Tom had called her a poster child.

"I hadn't thought about that." Her Canadian accent made it *aboot*. "What about the guard and the free room?"

"If you were mugged it would be bad publicity. And as for comping a room, if you wake up and feel like gambling some more, they may get some of their money back."

Alice shook her head. "I thought he was being nice."

"In Atlantic City, that *is* nice."

Her motel was two blocks off Pacific. "There's my room. Twenty-seven, eh?"

"Twenty-seven-A?"

"Just twenty-seven." She laughed. "My Canadian accent fooled you. The great Northern 'eh.' Why aren't we going in?"

I had circled the dark parking lot and was looking it over. "I'm supposed to protect you. Is there any chance Colin is here?"

"Him? Not likely. When do the baseball players leave?"

"Not for another hour."

"He'll be out until then, getting autographs." She snorted. "I wouldn't mind so much if it was *hockey*. At least that's Canadian."

We opened the car doors and were slammed by the heat. Who the hell said it could be this hot the first weekend in October? The beach season was supposed to be long over — that was one reason the casinos were holding events like the baseball festival.

"It's like an oven," said Alice. "I suppose you're used to it down here." If you live in Ontario, I guess New Jersey counts as the deep south.

At first I thought her room had been tossed. Suitcases lay open on the beds, their contents spread out in haphazard piles. But Alice was unruffled. She picked up a bra from the floor and looked thoughtful. "I'll have to separate our stuff. I don't want him to have any excuse to come looking for me."

I hid a sigh. This looked like an all-night job, and packing is not what I became a private eye for.

Alice had other plans. "I'm going to make up a list of things I'll need, Marty. You can buy them for me while I repack."

I frowned. "I'm not supposed to leave you."

She smiled. "Sweet, dependable Marty Crow." She put a hand on my arm. "A girl can always count on you, can't she?"

"I'm your bodyguard."

"The fact is, I need to write a note to that — that man. Telling him why he'll never see me again. Frankly, I'd prefer you weren't here while I do it. Go buy the things I need, Marty." She gave me a different smile. "I'll make it up to you later."

I have had a lot of women tell me to leave. I have had a few flirt with me. Alice was the first to do both at the same time.

Eventually I took her shopping list and left, first making her swear not to let anyone in and to call the cops if anything suspicious happened. "I'll be back in half an hour," I promised. Dependable Marty Crow.

Out in the sauna I cranked up my car's grouchy A.C. and listened to it complain as I drove back to Pacific Avenue. I remember sitting at the corner for a moment, watching the traffic that never died away completely, not even in the middle of the night. There was a Quickie-Mart a few blocks to the left, a supermarket half a mile to the right. I chose left.

And that's how easily things happen. Turn left instead of right and people's lives change all over the place, just as if a hurricane had come crashing onto the beach.

There were only two cars in the lot at the convenience store. Bad orchestra music buzzed woozily over the P.A. system and the manager behind the counter — middle-aged, thinning hair, and a half-hearted moustache — was scrapping hot dogs that been too long on the rollers.

I pulled out Alice's list and started through the aisles. Hair gel, bobby pins, nail clippers. Amazing what some people can't live without.

Someone brushed past me: a young black man wearing a red basketball jacket. In that weather that jacket would have killed me, but maybe his car's air conditioner worked better than mine. He was humming and bobbing to music in his head, music that clearly had no connection to the old show tune the in-store sound system was murdering.

I thought about Alice. Before I took off, her flirting had become more obvious, making it clear that she wanted me to stay in her room at the casino for more reasons than just protection.

I knew this wasn't because of my devastating charm; it was just a reaction to the break-up with Colin. But did that mean I was obligated to ignore it? She wasn't really a client; the casino would be getting my bill, not her. So why shouldn't we share some comfort on a hot night?

By the time I reached the counter I had myself convinced that she was fair game, so to speak. The manager seemed startled to see me, as if he'd forgotten I was in the place. "That all, Mister?"

"Yes, that's all." I paid with a credit card, figuring the bill would go to Rose Casino.

"Hot night, huh?"

"Yeah. Hot." I picked up two bags full of things Alice couldn't live without.

"Here's your receipt and card," said the manager, wedging them into my hand.

"Thanks." I backed out the door and walked to my car. But when I dumped the bags in my back seat I discovered that the manager had only given me the receipt. No credit card.

I sighed and started walking back across the lot toward the store. That's when I heard the gunshot.

The same people who would have told Alice I was not dependable would have assured her that when bullets fly I head the other way. They are generally right; I have way too much respect for life to risk my own.

But leaving my credit card at the scene of a robbery or worse didn't sound like the best plan I'd ever heard. If I had my cell phone with me I would have hit 911 and stayed out of the way, but the mobile phone company and I were having a little disagreement about billing terms.

I pulled the gun out of my shoulder holster and moved quickly up to the big front windows. When I reached the doorway I received a sight that would stay with me.

The manager, gun in hand, was leaning across the counter, staring at the black teenager who lay, jerking and twitching, face down on the floor. The manager must have heard me because he twisted around, pointing his pistol.

I dropped to the cement. "Hey, peace!" I shouted through the glass. "I heard the shots. You need any help?"

"Who are you?" His voice was shaky.

"I'm a private detective. Just happened to be passing by." It felt crazy, shouting back and forth through the doorway, but it would have been crazier to go in aiming guns at each other.

"What happened?" I called. "Was it a robbery?"

"Yeah. Punk pulled a gun on me."

I wiped sweat off my gun hand. "Okay if I come in?"

The manager gave a nervous laugh, as if the ridiculousness of the situation had suddenly caught up with him. "Sure, come on in."

I walked into the bright, cool, fluorescent space of the store. The manager had left his gun on the counter and was bending over the robber. "I think he's dead."

"You better call 911."

"Yeah. You keep an eye on things." He straightened up and headed back to the counter.

I looked down at the dead man. There was a gun lying on the robber's far side, close to his right hand. It was a cheap revolver, the kind the newspapers call a Saturday night special.

The manager hung up. "Cops are coming."

"Good. Now I have to make a call." I walked around the counter and picked up his phone. I would tell Alice about the delay, ask her to call Juarez and have the casino send someone else to her rescue.

I dialed the first four digits before I was interrupted.

"Mitch! My God, Mitch!"

I spun around, swinging my gun up. Another young man was standing in the doorway: a short, thin black man who stared in horror at the corpse on the floor.

His eyes were wide as he turned and saw my gun. "You killed him, you crazy man. What you do that for?"

"Put your hands behind your head. Do it!"

The young man raised his hands. "Oh, Mitch."

I made the kid kneel and patted him down for weapons. He was crying now. That didn't surprise me. I had seen hard men break down when their friends died, and even more who sobbed when they themselves were arrested.

The manager was gingerly carrying the dead robber's gun to the island in the middle of the room. He placed it on the counter, next to a six-pack of cola and a bag of potato chips. "I hear sirens."

"Oh, Mitch," said the kid. "Mitch, what did they do to you?"

Ever have a dream where everything goes in slow motion and you can't get anywhere, no matter how you try? That was the rest of my night.

By the time the Atlantic City detectives found the time to interview me I was ticked off. The first patrolman on the scene had taken my gun and driver's license and threatened to handcuff me when I tried to use the phone.

The next officers to arrive asked me a few questions and then tried to ignore me. I talked them into letting me at the pay phone, but the motel number was busy. I called the casino but Tom Juarez was off duty and his assistant didn't know me, didn't know about Alice, and didn't see any reason to locate her boss to find out more.

I was trying the motel again when the detectives arrived and sent me to the back of the store. The manager and the second black man had gone off to the police station while I remained in limbo. Now it was three damned A.M. and the detectives had finally deigned to talk to me.

"Let's go over this one more time, Crow," said the male detective. He was a beefy man with a blond crewcut, and had identified himself as Anquist.

I shook my head. "Not till I make a phone call."

The younger detective, a dark-haired woman named Shellcross, squinted at me. "Your lawyer?"

"For what? I didn't do anything. My gun was never fired."

"Kid could sue you for pointing a gun," Anquist said, more to himself than anything else. "Reckless endangerment. False imprisonment, maybe."

"You going to law school at night?" I guessed.

"Let's stick to the point," said Shellcross. "Mr. Crow, you're a licensed private investigator. That means you're a trained observer, right?"

I knew butter when somebody spread it on me. "I try."

"So where was Mitch Wainwright — that's the dead man — where was his gun, when you first looked in the door?"

"I didn't see it."

"Bingo," said Anquist, and then to his partner: "You see?"

"Doesn't prove anything," she said, irritably.

"Listen," I said. "Don't you think I could be more help if I knew what was going on?"

From the looks they exchanged I guessed they didn't.

I sighed. "Let's start with the obvious. The manager shot Wainwright. He says it was a robbery, right?"

The blond cop nodded.

"So, what's the problem? There's some hang-up or we'd all be home by now. Some glitch with his statement?"

"No," said Shellcross.

"Yes," said her partner.

"Great," I said. "That clears things right up."

Shellcross shrugged. "There's nothing wrong with Packer's story. That's the manager's name: Thomas Packer. But Anquist here wonders why you didn't see the gun when you first looked in —"

"I couldn't have. It was on the far side of the body."

"Yeah," said Anquist. "You told us that."

"You think the manager was lying? That it wasn't a robbery?"

Anquist frowned. "I'm not ready to close the file, is all I'm saying. Parts of this stink."

"So, where did the gun come from if it wasn't a

robbery?" asked Shellcross.

"Where did it come from if it *was?*" her partner retorted. "You think he carried it on the plane?"

"Hold it," said I. "You lost me again. The dead teenager, he just got off a plane?"

"This is according to Lamont Nelson, the kid you drew down on," Anquist explained. "He said Wainwright was his cousin from Seattle. Just flew in to Philly last night for a family wedding. It was his first time on this coast so Lamont took him to see the casinos."

"So did he bring the gun on the plane?" I asked. "It's a good question."

"Lamont Nelson, the cousin," said Shellcross. "He gave it to him. *He* didn't just get off a plane."

"So why the robbery?" said Anquist. "Since when is that how you welcome a cousin to the east coast? Take him out at night, hand him a gun, and tell him to rob a convenience store?"

"I don't," said his partner. "But I don't have a record like Lamont Nelson."

"Armed robbery?" I asked.

Anquist shook his head. "Joy-riding in a car somebody else stole. Drunk and disorderly. A screw-up, sure. But he's never been caught in possession of a gun, much less doing an armed robbery, for Gods' sake."

"Does Wainwright have a record back in Seattle?"

"Got a call in on that."

I sipped bad Quickie-Mart coffee. "You think the store manager panicked. Alone at night with a black teenager."

"The manager has been robbed twice in the last three years," said Anquist. "He bought the gun after the second time. Maybe he had himself so psyched up to use it he just *assumed* this was a robbery. That's been known to happen."

"Or maybe it really was one," said Shellcross. "If it

wasn't, where do you think the second gun came from?"

"It was a throwdown." Anquist looked at me to make sure I knew what that meant. "Some cops have been known to carry a second gun, or even a knife, just in case they shoot a guy and find out he didn't have a weapon."

"Yeah, I've heard of it."

"Not Atlantic City cops," said Shellcross, firmly.

"Heaven forbid," I said. "I take it fingerprints don't help."

Anquist nodded. "Wainwright's prints are on the gun, but if Packer put the gun down by the body he had time to set that up. No prints on the ammo."

"What does the manager say happened?"

Shellcross consulted her notebook. "Packer says that just after you left Wainwright came up to the counter with a six-pack of cola and a bag of potato chips.

"Packer bent down to get a paper bag and when he looked up Wainwright had a gun in his hand. He said: 'Give me all the money in the register. Put it in the bag with the soda and the chips.'

"Packer pulled his gun and told the kid to leave. He thought Wainwright was going to fire so he beat him to it." She looked up from the notebook. "It could have happened just like that."

"*If* Wainwright had a gun," said Anquist. "If —"

"Wait a minute." I was frowning. "There's something wrong with that story."

"Yeah? What?"

"I don't know." I stared up at the fluorescent lights. Why didn't I just let it go? I needed to get back to Alice, before her Toronto boyfriend tired of chasing ballplayers . . .

Toronto.

My Canadian accent, eh?

I looked at the soda and the potato chips, still sitting

on the counter. The answer had been there all night long, waiting for me to understand it.

"Was that a quote?" I asked. "I mean, the manager claims that what you just told me is what Wainwright said to him?"

"Supposed to be. So?"

"So it never happened. Not like that."

"You mean Wainwright didn't have the gun?"

"For all I know he had a Sherman tank and a flame thrower. But he never said what you told me he said."

They were both frowning. "Why not?"

"Because Wainwright was from Seattle, Washington. And that means he never asked the manager to put the soda in a bag."

"Why not?" asked Shellcross. "They don't drink soda in Seattle?"

"That's right. They don't."

The cops looked as if they had joined the crowd who didn't think I was dependable.

"Listen," I said. "I spent a week in Washington state last year looking for a casino executive."

"Embezzler?" guessed Anquist.

"Nope. One of the Indian tribes was setting up a casino out there. They invited him as a consultant. No one at home had heard from him since."

"Did you find him?"

"Yeah. He'd gone native, so to speak. Built himself a teepee and was living in the dirt. He was preaching to the Indians; telling them to reject the White man's filthy gambling habit. The tribe was thrilled when I showed up; they had been trying to find someone to collect him. One guy told me: 'you fellas spent two hundred years trying to make us be White. Now you want to tell us how to be Indian.'"

"This is all fascinating," said Shellcross, but she was lying. "Does it have anything to do with a dead man in

Atlantic City?"

"Just this," I told her. "I found out that in Washington state they don't drink soda. They drink pop."

Anquist frowned. "You mean *soda* pop."

"Right. But *we* call it soda and *they* call it pop. Plus, a lot of people there call a paper bag a sack. And scrap paper they call scratch paper."

Shellcross looked ready to punch somebody. "What the hell does scrap paper have to do with this case?"

"Nothing," I admitted. "I just thought it was interesting."

"Wrong again. You're saying that this guy Wainwright, being from Seattle, wouldn't have told the manager to put the soda in a bag. He would have said, 'put the pop in a sack.'"

"Exactly."

She shook her head. "That's awfully thin. Are we supposed to take your word for it?"

"Call Princeton. There must be somebody in the language department who knows about regional English."

Anquist looked a lot happier. "Damn. I knew Packer was lying. Thanks a lot, Crow."

"My pleasure," I said. "Now I'll just be going —"

"Not till we call the university," said Shellcross. "We may need you to talk to them."

Oh hell. "Look. Let me try to call my client again."

"Sure." She waved toward the phone. "Make yourself at home."

This time I reached the motel. "She checked out," the clerk told me.

"Somebody from the casino came for her?"

"No. It was her fiancé, I guess."

"You guess? Are you sure?"

"Well, I think so. She was hanging all over him. Said they were going back to Canada to get married today."

I guess Colin didn't look so bad after I stood her up. Maybe that was all for the best.

"Say," said the clerk. "Is your name, uh, Crow?"

"That's right."

"She left a message here for you."

"Read it to me, would you?"

"Sure." He shuffled paper. "It says, 'you slimy little —'"

There was a long pause. When he spoke again the clerk sounded a little different. "I don't think I should read this over the phone."

"You're probably right," I said. We hung up.

Outside, a police car pulled into traffic, cutting off a taxi. The cab veered left and sideswiped an SUV. Horns honked in rage.

Pacific Avenue was greeting the dawn.

Lobster Bisque

Tim Wohlforth

Hollow eyes, short blonde hair in disarray, white shirt and jeans covered with food stains. Laura Simmons looked like she hadn't slept in a week. I remembered her as a plump, cheerful young woman. She used to work part-time in the kitchen at Big Emma's, the bar on Jack London Square. I used that place as my office. A private investigator doesn't need anything elaborate.

Laura now worked at *La Provence,* Oakland's newest, priciest restaurant. Written up in the *New York Times.* Two month's wait for a reservation.

It was ten in the morning. Where had she been all night? If she went home after her restaurant job, she hadn't bothered to shower or change her clothes. So unlike her. Neat, well organized, hardworking.

"What's this all about, Laura? You said it was an emergency."

We shared a table in front of Green's Organic Coffee on College Avenue. Half a block from *La Provence.*

"Jim, I feel I'm going to be charged with murder."

"Whose?"

"Carol Smythe."

"You're kidding. *The* Carol Smythe?"

World famous chef. Owner of *La Provence*. Four-page spread in this month's *Gourmet Magazine*. I knew a little too much about Symthe. Some say she was better at self-promotion than cooking.

"None other."

"So what happened?"

"You don't know her. She was a hellion to work for. Tough. Insulting. Impossible to satisfy. Despite her reputation, her staff passed through a revolving door. I'm good. Worked in the best restaurants in town. Figured some day I'd have my own place. I worked my butt off for her. I tried. God, I tried. Needed her reference. A step up for me."

"And?"

"Last night I made this lobster bisque. But I didn't follow Smythe's recipe exactly. Added just a touch of fresh thyme simmered gently in butter, paprika, and heavy cream. Used fresh Maine lobster. Blanched, not pre-cooked. Perfect. Carol came over and tasted it. She knew it was fabulous. That was the problem. It was better than hers. She started cursing me. 'You stupid, fat bitch,' she shouted. The rest of the kitchen staff stopped and watched us. 'You've ruined my bisque. Wouldn't feed it to hogs. Where did you work last? Wendy's?'"

"Sounds like a sick, competitive lady."

Who says talented celebrities were nice people? Perhaps *People Magazine*. But, in my experience, it ain't necessarily so. Some couldn't be sweeter. But there were just as many mean bastards. Maybe more.

"I knew that coming in. I figured I could handle the abuse. Keep my mouth shut and learn. But the rage grew inside me, Jim. And the pressure. Last night was just too much. Wouldn't have minded if the bisque was ruined. But it was the best I've ever tasted. Four star. I wanted to kill her on the spot."

I felt as she felt. Rage within me against this arrogant woman who had treated her so miserably. Laura's cooking was more than a way to make a living. It was her life. Like a painter's canvases, an author's books. Smythe's remarks had cut deep into Laura's soul.

"Did you kill her?" I asked. I might have.

"I couldn't have. I'm not a killer. But I wanted to. I took the large stockpot of bisque and poured it down the drain. 'I quit,' I shouted at her and stormed out of the place."

Laura hadn't touched her latté. I took a sip of mine. Then looked out over the peaceful Oakland scene. Upscale area. Far away from my haunts down by the marina at Jack London Square. A morning crowd of women with strollers, retirees, college types with books under their arms, and kids on skateboards playing hooky. Mainly white.

"What time was it?"

"Five o'clock. The place doesn't open till six."

"Then what did you do?"

"I went for a long walk. For miles. Had a bite to eat at a Cambodian restaurant on University Avenue. Then ended up at the Berkeley Marina. The fresh breeze off the bay helped to clear my head. I told myself it was all for the best. I was ready to move on. Carol knew I was too good to be just a sous-chef."

"That's a lot of walking."

"I know. I just had to clear my head. It started to get cold out on the pier. So I walked all the way home. I live near here. Just collapsed. Didn't change clothes. At six this morning the cops knocked on my apartment door."

"And told you Smythe was dead?"

"That's right. Happened around eleven last night. At the restaurant."

"They found the body that quick? How did they manage that?"

"Didn't tell me. But I figured it was the cleaning crew. Came in every night after midnight to vacuum. Carol was a nut on cleanliness."

"And you have no alibi for eleven o'clock."

"Fast asleep at home. By myself. And ten people saw me arguing with Carol."

"That's all they have?"

"There's more. The cops said she was killed by someone who stuffed her head into a boiling pot of lobster bisque. Like the soup we argued over. Her head red as a lobster. Grotesque look on her face."

She started to cry.

"Who could kill someone like that?" she continued. "Even a person like Carol? I couldn't have."

"I thought you dumped the soup."

"I did. Guess she made another batch."

"They took your fingerprints?"

"Yes."

"And you suspect they may find your fingerprints on the pot."

"Or the stove, utensils. It's my work station."

She stared at me with her tear-swollen, puffy eyes. Imploring me to help her.

"What do you want me to do?"

"Find Carol's killer. Otherwise they'll stick me with it. I'll pay you."

"Suppose I find out it was you after all?"

"I couldn't kill like that. Only a madman could."

She started crying again. Now she was a real mess. Red eyes and nose. Dirty cheeks streaked with rivulets of tears. A child in a grown-up's body. I couldn't say no.

"Can you suggest any other suspects?"

"Most anybody working in the kitchen."

"Anyone who has had a recent argument with her?"

"Roger Allegre. He's the sous-chef in charge of the

grill. A master with the chafing dish. Fish. Reduction sauces. Had a row with Carol a couple of nights ago. She claimed his fish was raw on the inside. Not possible with Roger. He was just getting too good for her. So she had to put him in his place."

"Anyone else?"

"Adriene Whitney."

"Come on. She's a bigger name than Smythe."

Creator of California Cuisine. Author of a dozen cookbooks. A regular on the *Today Show.* Friend of our former president. Sponsor of organic gardens in poor East Oakland neighborhoods.

"Smythe used to work for her. The rumor is that she stole most of her recipes from Whitney. Then Smythe turns around and attacks Adriene in her interview in *Gourmet*. Said Adriene had fallen into a rut. Lost her creative edge."

"This Smythe lady was something else."

"Yes. But she didn't deserve to be boiled red like a lobster."

Roger Allegre lived in a small second floor apartment accessed through outside stairs. A cozy place with flowerpots filled with azaleas seated along the railing of the back porch.

I glanced in the glass window of the door before I knocked. It opened into a small and exceedingly messy kitchen. Dishes piled up in the sink. An open jar of peanut butter on the counter. burned toast by the stove. Suggested that Allegre saved his cooking energy for work. And that he was a bachelor.

I knocked. A thin man, perhaps thirty, approached the door. Dripping wet. He wore a white stained tank top and gray sweats. Muscular, a tattoo of a M-16 rifle ran along one arm from his bulging bicep to his wrist. A dagger with a bloody tip covered his other forearm. Short, spiked, shiny dyed-black hair. A tough customer. Or so he wished to be perceived.

"I gave at the office," he said with a smirk as he opened the door.

"It's your office I want to talk about."

"Wise guy."

He lifted a fist and prepared to strike. I gave him a kick in the chest and rushed in the door. He sprawled on the floor. Not so tough, after all. I pulled out my .38 and pointed it at his skull.

"I don't like to be threatened," I said. "I mean you no harm. Just have a couple of questions about *La Provence.*"

"Who are you?" he said, holding his stomach. "You're no cop. They come in pairs. Anyway they were here an hour ago."

"Private. Name's Jim Wolf."

"Working for?"

"Laura."

"Ah," he smiled. "She killed her, you know. And I don't blame her."

"Let's talk about it."

He stood and led me into his small, cluttered living room, dominated by a set of weights and a stationary bicycle. Body building magazines covered the coffee table. The place stank of sweat and mineral oil. I pushed aside a copy of the *San Francisco Chronicle* opened to the sports page and plopped down on his soiled black leather couch. Roger dropped into a matching chair opposite me. I placed my gun back in its shoulder holster. Roger glared at me. Not a very likable fellow.

"What makes you say Laura killed her?" I asked.

"Because I would have if I'd been her. The way Carol

treated her was criminal. Justifiable homicide I'd call it. And that lobster bisque business. Was Laura pissed. Rightly so. She let me sip it before the Dragon Lady came over for an imperial taste. Fantastic. Laura has the touch. Carol knew it."

"That's why she picked on Laura?"

"Carol remembers what she did to Whitney. Didn't want any of us doing the same to her."

"And you?"

"Me what?"

"You had no love for Carol."

"Laura tell you that? Some friend."

"Friendship doesn't seem to be in large supply in restaurant kitchens."

"You have that right. War zones. Pressure. Personal rivalries. To top it off, unless you're on Carol's level, the pay stinks."

"You didn't answer my question," I said. "What was your relationship with Carol?"

"Shitty. Like everybody else. I ran that place. Not Carol. She did the PR and took the bows. The grill station's the heart of any quality restaurant. I cooked the steaks, fish, created reduction sauces to order. Food went from my station straight to the customer's table. A matter of timing, skill."

"And Carol didn't appreciate you?"

"Oh, she knew what she had in me. I made that restaurant for her. I was too damned good for her. So she did her best to keep me down. Said I serve raw fish. Bullshit."

"Did you kill her?"

He jumped up from his chair and lunged for me. Rage in his eyes. Caught me by surprise. He grabbed me by the throat and squeezed. Strong bastard.

I gasped for air. Tried to pull his hands from my neck.

Like a vise. Tightening. Hands didn't budge. I flailed at the bastard, scratching at his arms. I began to black out. Then he relaxed his grip and laughed.

"By the door," he said. "That was a lucky kick."

He retreated back to his chair. I sat for a moment, breathing heavily. My throat still hurt. Nothing would make me happier than to stick this murder on him. He had the strength, the temper, and the motivation. He could be the killer. Almost killed me.

I was about to jump the muscled-bound punk again. Could have flattened him with another karate kick. He was all testosterone. No skill. But thought better of it. I was falling into a macho battle with an asshole. Not why I came there. I took my gun out of its holster and placed it within easy reach on my lap.

"I could have done it," he said, reading my thoughts.

He gave me a sickly superior smile. Like he had won because I had to retreat to using my gun. Let him think what he wanted. The more confident he felt, the more likely he would be to slip up.

"Thought about it many times," he continued. "But Laura beat me to it. Didn't think fatso had it in her."

"But you do."

"What?"

"Have it in you to kill."

"I'll tell you one thing."

"Yes?"

"If I had killed her, I wouldn't have dunked her head in a pot of lobster bisque. I'd have pushed her arrogant face into a chafing dish filled with sizzling hot oil."

I waited until five o'clock to walk into *Chez Étienne*, Adriene Whitney's world-famous bistro in North Berkeley.

Easy to miss. The restaurant occupied a modest brown-shingled house, covered with vines, set back from a busy commercial street. You had to know it was there or you'd walk right by. Gourmands world around knew it was there.

I passed under an ivy-covered trellis and entered the restaurant. I brushed past the maître d', muttering something about an appointment, and headed into the kitchen in the rear. A small area, packed with a half-dozen earnest young men and women prepping their stations.

"I'm looking for Adriene," I said to a petite pastry chef covered with flour. She was rolling a long tube of dough.

"The office at the end on the left," she answered as she reached for a large knife and began slicing the dough into inch-thick cylinders.

I followed her directions and entered a cluttered space packed with cookbooks in several languages. Whitney sat behind a desk piled high with slips of papers. She didn't look up, absorbed in scratching a recipe on a sheet of paper with a large inlaid-gold, marbled fountain pen. Every now and then she would touch the tip of the pen to her stained tongue. Not a good habit.

"How can I help you?" she asked in a cultured voice with a slight French lilt to it. She had noticed me. Wavy richly-gray hair, fine bright red lips, inquiring green eyes. White silk blouse, gray skirt, matching jacket on the back of her chair.

"I'm Jim Wolf, a private investigator. I've been asked to look into the death of Carol Smythe. I thought you might be able to help fill me in about her background. I understand she once worked for you."

"Horrible. The radio announcer said something about an irate employee pushing her head into a pot of lobster bisque. Hard to believe."

"Why is it so hard to believe?"

"Oh, I suppose Carol had a way of irritating people. I

heard the rumors. The restaurant community in this area is incestuous. But putting her head into a pot of simmering soup? A sacrilege."

Was the killing a sacrilege? Or ruining the soup?

"I hear she stole her main recipes from you."

Adriene smiled warmly. She shrugged her shoulders and waved her hands at the books and papers surrounding her.

"She was welcome to them. I publish most of them in books. I have no secrets." She reached above her and pinched the air. "You cannot steal what is here. Great cooking is not a formula. There is technique. There are the proper quantities of ingredients. Heats and times. If that was all there was to it, any first-year chemistry student could be a great cook."

"Then what is it?"

"Magic." She pinched the air again and winked at me. "Magic dust."

"Are you serious?"

"Couldn't be more so. My mother was a Frenchwoman, a marvelous cook. My father an Englishman, a professor of religion. I owe my father as much as my mother for my cooking skills, such as they are."

"So you didn't resent Carol's borrowing from you."

"She didn't borrow from me. I've eaten at her restaurant. Same recipes. Entirely different effect. Not bad. No, not bad."

"Then she turned around and attacked you in *Gourmet Magazine.*"

"That attack reflected on her, not me. I do not fear my reputation."

"So you wished Carol no harm?"

"You think I killed her?" She laughed. "You do not understand me or what I try to do with my cooking."

"I assume you want to be the best there is. I would

certainly have resented such an attack, especially coming from someone who owed you so much."

"You are not me. For me it is not a competition. I cook because I must. I was placed in this world to cook. When I succeed with a dish, I know why." She pinched the air again. "It is not me. It is the dust."

As she talked of magic dust, her green eyes glowed, her accent thickened. Maybe she was a magician pretending to be a chef. But a murderer? Awfully hard to believe.

"And I would never commit an act of violence," she continued. "My whole life is dedicated to one aim only."

"And that is?'

"Peace."

Ah, Berkeley. I had expected an answer like that. Whitney must be worth millions, yet she was as Berkeley as a homeless street punk riding a skateboard on Telegraph Avenue. There was an invisible line, rarely even marked with a sign, that separated Berkeley from Oakland and the rest of the world. I preferred Oakland despite its high crime rate, pockets of poverty, drugs and gangs. Oakland was real. Berkeley a dream. Yet, as they say about New York City, it was a nice place to visit.

I thanked Adriene for her help and headed back to my hometown three miles away. Had she been helpful? Not really. I wasn't much into magic dust. If there was the kind of rage inside her needed to shove Carol's head into boiling bisque, she sure as hell was good at hiding it.

Somehow my visit with the spiritual Adriene unsettled me. The death of Carol Smythe became all the more gruesome. My mind was flooded with the image of a woman's face, red as a cooked lobster, contorted by pain, remnants of soup dripping from her hair. No person, no matter how cruel she may be herself, deserved such a death.

Then it came to me. Something about lobster. I

needed to talk with Laura again.

We found the same table in front of Green's Organic Coffee. The street bustled with the after-work crowd heading for home, bookstores, restaurants.

"So how's it going?" Laura asked. She had showered and changed her clothes. Yet her face was drawn, expressionless. Like she'd given up on life. I knew she hadn't slept.

"Forget about Adriene Whitney," I said. "Her response to attacks appears to be to sprinkle the perpetrator with magic dust."

"And you believe her?"

"I've never been into magic myself. But, yes, I believe her."

"How about Roger?"

"Different animal entirely. And I mean animal."

"He has his rough edges."

"He could be Smythe's killer. Nearly killed me."

"So what are you going to do?"

"I could make as good a case against him as the cops seem to be trying to make against you. But I won't."

"Why not?"

"Because you killed Carol Smythe."

I expected her to explode. Or maybe run. She did neither. It was like she was prepared for the accusation. She cast her eyes downward. Her shoulders slumped. I thought she would fall off her chair.

"You're supposed to be on my side," she muttered without conviction.

"I warned you I would take this thing wherever it led me."

"Why do you think I did it?"

"Because of a red lobster."

"Lobster?"

"This morning you told me that Carol's face was red like a cooked lobster."

"I may have."

"How did you know?"

"The cops told me."

She continued to speak to the table, not me. I had trouble catching her words.

"They couldn't have because her face wouldn't have been red by the time they saw it."

"How do you know?"

"My trade. As a PI, my bread and butter work is insurance. I get called in at accident scenes all the time. Attend autopsies. I know bodies. Let's figure the cops saw the body between two and three hours after the murder. After thirty minutes postmortem lividity sets in. The blood, no longer pumped by a working heart, drains from areas like the face and accumulates in lower areas. Where it accumulates, it turns purple. Even if blood had flowed to her face, it would have been purple, not red."

"You sure?"

"Yes. Something else. You said she had a look of horror on her face. It's a myth that victims retain the expression they assumed at the time of death. Within minutes the muscles in the facial area relax. The face becomes expressionless."

I almost added "like your face is now."

"The only person to see Carol," I continued, "with a lobster red face frozen in horror was the killer. You."

She nodded and started to cry. I knew an image of the dead Carol's face had returned to her mind. If it had ever left her.

"How could I have killed her? I mean I told you this morning that she must have been killed by a madman. You think I am mad?"

"Are you saying you didn't do it?"

"I'm saying I don't know. That's why I hired you. I guess I must have. I should have told you the whole story this morning. It's just that it didn't seem real. More like a nightmare. I hoped you would prove it was all just a bad dream."

"You better explain."

She sat there for a moment, shaking, face now swollen from tears, nose running. I wanted to reach out to her. But couldn't. She was the killer.

"I went for the walk just like I said." She began to speak slowly in a monotone. "Then, on my way home, I remembered I had left my set of knives at the restaurant. Carol was there. She laughed at me. Said she would see to it that I never worked again in the industry. I noticed a simmering stockpot of lobster bisque on the stove. Since it was featured on the menu she must have made it after I left yesterday afternoon. Taunted me to taste it. I came toward her. There was this rage inside me. God, I hated that bitch. Next thing I remember she was lying on the floor staring up at me, face red like a lobster, contorted by pain, eyes accusing me. I ran."

Maybe she was insane when she killed. I'd leave that question to experts, to the jury. But kill she did. And horribly.

"You going to turn me in?" she asked.

"Of course."

"She deserved it."

"No one deserves to die as Carol died."

"I . . . I know."

"Here's the name of a good lawyer."

I handed her Sandra Jacobs' card. The best defense lawyer in the Bay Area. Laura would need her. I got up and left Laura sitting there. I walked down the street past the shuttered *La Provence,* wrapped up in yellow crime tape.

Like a Christmas package. I headed toward Wendy's.

It would be awhile before I would be able to eat lobster bisque again.

The Ice Princess

D. Jeanette McSherry

August, 2001, 6:15 A.M.
Houston, Texas

Private Detective Joe Henderson stared at his partner's shapely rear in a feeble attempt to escape the grotesque parody the Gourmet Gutter had left in his wake. Not even Prussia's hourglass figure could compete with the carnage. Seven months — seven victims, wined and dined — then gutted. Each corpse gruesomely displayed in an isolated setting, complete with edible props.

Prussia Ice tilted her head as she squatted in front of the corpse, as curious and intent as a sleek, golden cat absorbed with its prey. Sunlight streamed over her, exaggerating every rippling movement in striking contrast to the disemboweled remains of the young woman. The victim met the Gutter's criteria: blonde, beautiful, and barely old enough to drink.

After nine weeks on the case, this was the first body recovered short of twelve hours. That probably explained the air of optimistic excitement pervading the crime scene. The killer was becoming bolder. This time he'd left the body in open view less than two miles off one of the main freeways encircling Houston.

Mud sucked and slurped at Joe's boots as he circled the crime scene with his Coolpix 996, then snapped off a roll with his old Nikon EL. The process was equal parts habit, nostalgic sentiment, and superstitious dread but he still occasionally found something in the darkroom that didn't show up with the digital.

Ducking beneath some low-hanging vines, Joe dodged a young officer running for the bushes. The sound of vomiting corkscrewed an almost tangible tension into the rest of the team. Someone chuckled, apparently trying to break the ice with some old-fashioned dark humor. No one was going to sleep well after today. Not until the Gutter was put out of commission.

Prussia remained riveted to the ghoulish display case. The body was arranged on a stump, the victim's back against a tree, appendages wired and tied to emulate a sophisticated dining pose: legs crossed, one arm in lap, the other daintily holding a champagne glass. A half empty bottle of vintage champagne was propped nearby. Like its predecessors, the corpse was naked, its chest crudely sutured.

Al Schivolsky, Chief of Detectives for the Houston Homicide Division, had recommended Joe to the last victim's family. Over a decade earlier, when Joe was still with the Bureau, they'd worked together on a high profile kidnapping. Since then, they had become close friends.

Like most wealthy families, the Wilsons expected more expedient results than the HPD could deliver. That's where Henderson & Ice came in. For a price, they could give Alice Wilson's murder their exclusive attention, something the police could not. Contrary to popular belief, private investigators don't get a crack at many homicides. When he scored a case like this, Joe's staff of part-timers managed the business while he and Prussia hunted monster.

Joe sighed with relief when the police photographer finished. Schivolsky cleared the scene and gave him the go-ahead. Prussia turned and met his gaze. Hers still held the innate curiosity of a researcher although academia hadn't been enough to satisfy her need to make a difference. "Find anything?" he asked, stretching and yawning like a waking grizzly.

Prussia ignored him. "Too early to tell. No defensive cuts, bruises, zip. Aside from the fatal wound, there's a puncture wound on her right arm. Think she was drugged?"

Joe ambled closer. "She doesn't look like a user. We'll have to wait for the pathology report." He clicked off four more shots. "Drugs would open up a new can of worms."

Prussia brushed past Joe like a fragrant breeze. "No evidence of cannibalism or necrophilia," she said. "And aside from the Wilson case, the killer hasn't indulged in excessive mutilation."

Joe flashed Prussia what she called his King Kong smile. "Yea, I think we can rule out most of the wilder sexual deviancies. Our psychopath is too methodical to be psychotic."

Schivolsky waved Prussia over, including her in the pow-wow between H&I's expert and the Department's Chief Forensic Officer. While she was gone, Joe scanned the crime scene a full 360, earning his nickname, Wide Angle. The Gutter's latest backdrop looked like something out of an old horror movie. Tangled woody vines hung from a jungle of canopied trees. Just past dawn, slimy fog banks hovered over the river in uneven patches like gray shape shifters looking for a place to land. Staged — perfectly for the find.

If only shadows could talk. Surely the fear vapors of sudden, violent death would remain to haunt this river until the monster was brought to justice. The area had been badly flooded less than a week before and large stagnant pools, some deep enough to swallow the rented Cavalier, surrounded the tragic waste of human life. Joe was no stranger to the smell of death, but it was somehow worse here in the heat and humidity. He was used to the depersonalization of city streets and the death masks of drug addicts, bums, thieves and whores . . . not the innocent creamy flesh of maidenly angels.

Joe circumnavigated the body, examining it from every angle, including the view from the victim's perspective. He measured the distance between the main road and the turnoff into this neck of the woods. What would bring a man here? A lone vendor, digging up crawdaddies along the riverbank, had discovered the body. Otherwise, it would have remained hidden like the others, for weeks, maybe even months.

Joe flipped an internal switch, adjusting his perspective to telephoto. The crime scene was only the first step in solving a case. You had to think like a killer — get into his head right down to the books he read and movies he watched in order to gain insight into his collective experience. Joe expected the autopsy on this victim would match the Gutter's M.O.

The murder weapon didn't have to be available to betray a killer's education and exposure. The Gutter's choice of weapon, a surgical saw, reflected a determination to refine his skills. He had become proficient at breaking the rib cage, extracting the heart and suturing the chest cavity. On occasion he'd been creative with other internal organs.

Oddly enough, the Gutter's methodology mimicked fiction although he didn't fit any known profile. A stream of bad slasher films and thrillers flashed through Joe's memory as he allowed the Gutter's experiences to seep into him. His bulk shuddered as he set aside personal morality to emulate a predator.

Each successive murder had become more exacting — well thought out and flawlessly executed. The Gutter didn't use excessive force. Instead he took his time, relishing the experience like a good meal. Food was definitely a prime incentive or catalyst.

Prussia's eyes flashed, startling Joe back into himself. He'd seen that look before — she was onto something. Once Prussia picked up the scent, she became as relentless as a bloodhound. She walked toward him through the drape of verdant jungle — even in boots, moving with the silky grace of a big cat. Damn! How she managed to stash her piece beneath those skintight slacks was beyond him.

Prussia ignored his appraising glance. "Last night was a full moon," she said, as if that explained everything. "He's like a werewolf, except he hunts all month long. He'll be looking for new prey tonight."

Four years working with Prussia had taught Joe that her hunches were rarely wrong. He liked to think himself the backbone of Henderson Investigations, but truth be told — Prussia was its heart. She felt things in her bones, not in some mumbo-jumbo supernatural way, but by getting outside herself into the victim's perspective. Joe understood the phenomena — a temporary break with reality similar to entering a killer's mind. Cops and PIs had one thing in common — to be good, you had to be part psychic.

"Have a name on her yet?" Prussia asked.

"No positive identification, but there's a missing person report on a Jacquelyn Wellington. The description matches. Beth is sending over a picture." H&I gave top billing to their few homicide cases, a luxury the police rarely had. "How'd your interview with the Wilsons go?"

Their clients had been vacationing in Europe when Prussia arrived in Houston.

She grimaced. "Weird. You were right. Martha and I could be sisters. I think I creeped her out, too — reminding her of Alice."

It had to be rough. Prussia's uncanny resemblance to the victims was probably the worst part of this job. Joe knew she dreaded meeting the families — looking into haunted, dead eyes that suddenly came alive when they saw her. "Martha may be the key," Joe said. "She knew the first suspect, Mark Somers. He had one prior for assault but no history of sex related crimes. Suddenly, three of the killings pointed to him."

"You're using past tense," Prussia said.

"Appropriately. Somers was killed during a high-speed car chase. Everyone assumed, incorrectly, we had our man until the fourth body was found."

"Where does Martha fit in?" Prussia asked.

"She dated Somers in high school. Jilted him. He didn't take it well. At the time the theory was — he was killing the girls because they reminded him of Martha."

"Just because the police had the wrong suspect doesn't disprove the motive. One of Martha's jilted beaus could be our man," Prussia said.

Prussia smiled. Joe had witnessed the subtle change in her features before. Once she made a connection — the pieces would start fitting together.

"I'm going to play things differently tonight. Dangling myself in front of this guy like something he can't have isn't going to do it. We've been waiting for him to hunt. Maybe he's not into a challenge."

Joe hadn't seen this coming. It was his own fault, encouraging Prussia's rogue side just because he'd never played by the book himself. "Organized killers don't favor one-night stands. The courtship is part of the fun," he objected.

"You're afraid I'll draw too much attention to myself and blow the sting," Prussia said.

"Maybe. We should also consider the fact that our guy is looking for younger prey. He could pass you up despite your resemblance to his past victims."

Prussia shot him a lethal look before she joined the coroner. Joe took the opportunity to pump the evidence team. Fingerprints were too much to hope for, but even a single clue could turn the tide.

Schivolsky motioned him over. "Henderson — Preston Lee, Victoria Sheriff's Department, Special Investigations Unit. They handled the Wilson case."

Joe offered his hand but Lee ignored the gesture. "Joe's running interference with the Wilsons," Schivolsky continued. "They want someone on their daughter's murder twenty-four-seven. Off the record, Joe here's got the specialization and funding we just don't have."

Lee strutted arrogantly around the body, devouring the girl's nakedness. "Then y'all must know, Alice met some friends at the Barnacle the weekend before she was murdered. Our boy is one clever son-of-a-gun, always meet'n his victims in public places."

From Schivolsky's glowing reports, Joe hadn't expected a fair-haired brown-noser with a honeyed smile and southern drawl. The cop reeked of bigot. Considering Lee's eyes were glued to Prussia, he obviously preferred blue-eyed blondes with peaches and cream complexions. Joe resented Prussia being treated as little more than eye candy. The HPD wasn't their turf, nor were the natives all that friendly to PIs, let alone beautiful, stubborn women.

"My men are spread pretty thin," Schivolsky said. "We have surveillance on over a dozen bars and malls. Unfortunately, The Barnacle is a good forty minutes from where they found the Wilson girl's body. I can't spare the manpower."

"So you want Ice and me to stake it out?" Joe asked.

"On the record? I never asked."

"The little lady's a dead ringer for Molly," Lee drawled, staring at Ice the way a starving man looks at food.

Joe bristled. "Who?"

"Martha Wilson. I've known the family a long time," Lee replied, edging closer to the victim. "Poor Alice had been dead a good forty-eight hours before we found her. I truly don't know which is worse. Seeing that — or this." Lee pointed to the Gutter's signature, the small, round metal tag attached to the girl's left breast. It read: 100% Angus Beef. Several local steak houses used them. "Ah, Louis Roederer, one of the few houses that still chooses to use skin maceration," Lee said, inhaling the aroma of the champagne. "An excellent choice."

Joe rolled his eyes at Schivolsky and tuned into Prussia's conversation with the coroner. "Hypostasis indicates she was moved less than six hours ago. Considering the condition of the body, he must have kept her on ice until then."

Joe's beeper went off. Excusing himself, he headed back to the car to take the call. Beth had worked her magic. A grainy picture of the missing girl awaited him on the laptop — a redhead. A shadow fell over his notebook. Joe looked up into Ice's shaded eyes. Nodding towards the body, he said, "Well, it's not Wellington."

Prussia's eyebrows rose. A smile crept over her face as she studied the picture. "Oh, it's her, Joe. I thought her hair smelled funny — like it had just been dyed. Don't you see? The Gutter needed to murder a blonde."

"So he changed her hair color back?" Joe smiled for the first time all day, comforted that good old-traditional investigative work might actually bring down this monster. Joe dialed the office to check if any other cosmetic changes might have been overlooked and find out when Jacquelyn had dyed her hair red. Joe added a few notes to the killer's computer-generated profile while they waited for Beth to check the records and reviewed the original background check run on Wellington: middle class, single, white, female. To this he added: Blonde. Blue eyes.

Prussia was shivering.

"You okay?" he asked. "Somebody walk over your grave?"

"My head is throbbing. Aside from that and a horribly disemboweled corpse — I'm just peachy."

Lee seemed more intrigued with Prussia than in doing his job. "Take a picture — it'll last longer," he mumbled. Lee didn't hear.

Prussia followed his eyes. "Don't waste your breath, Joe. Let's catch a few winks while the pathologist does his thing. They'll be moving her soon anyway. We can meet at the morgue around five."

Finally wresting his eyes from Prussia, Lee turned his attention back to the corpse. "Sick bastard," Joe muttered, watching the Detective savor the spectacle the way one might examine the clarity and aroma of a fine wine.

Prussia turned. "You do that — when you're trying to get into a perv's head."

He shot Prussia a glare. He didn't feast on death with such inhuman relish. Unconsciously, Joe patted his .38 Smith & Wesson and glanced in the back seat at the sawed off pump with pistol grip neatly rolled into his jacket. "Miss Wellington," he whispered, "give us something we can use."

"Too bad we can't depend on the Gutter to gift us his DNA," Prussia said. "What good is technology when what you really need is some good old fashioned luck."

"Look on the bright side. We didn't have the benefit of examining the other bodies this soon." Joe sighed.

"He wined and dined her. Then he screwed and gutted her. This guy has one heck of an unpleasant association with food. You'd think someone this deranged would relish his victim's fear and agony."

Ignoring the ugly, jagged gash traveling from between the victim's breasts to her belly, Joe studied the girl's eyes. Now a milky shade of blue, he imagined them filled with life and sparkling like Yogo sapphires.

Prussia turned towards the victim. "Some drugs can incapacitate and still leave the central nervous system receptive to pain. If his motive is revenge, the girls must remind him of someone who made one helluvan impression — hurt him in a way he couldn't forget. Someone brought out the beast."

Prussia didn't usually connect with the killer like this. That was his job. "Find anything to add to his profile?" Joe asked.

"He has the time to get to know his victims . . . play with their heads and emotions. Marriage would cramp his style. Since several of the girls frequented the Barnacle, I would guess he lives nearby. He made mistakes when he went out of his territory, for instance, the partial tire print we recovered in the Manfield case."

"The first bodies we found weren't as elaborately displayed. Why do you think he changed his M.O. midstream?" Joe asked.

"I think Alice Wilson was his *coup de grâce.*"

Joe nodded, remembering the macabre display case — pheasant under glass and a half empty bottle of Cristal Rose 95. "More props. More sadistic. He sure gave her special treatment."

Prussia grimaced. "You make special treatment sound like a good thing."

Joe shook his head sadly.

"My gut tells me Alice went under the knife without

benefit of drugs," Prussia continued. "The way he displayed her says it all. She pissed him off. She didn't scream or cry or beg for her life. He didn't get any while she was alive — but she got a little piece of him. Alice fought for her life. She bit him, Joe! Probably left us one healthy sample of that bastard's DNA under her nails too — that's why he deposited her teeth in a half-full champagne glass and cut off her hands!"

"Earth to Prussia. Come back to me, Ice."

Prussia tweaked his cheek. "Don't worry, Joe. Tonight The Gourmet Gutter is going to mess with the wrong girl."

Although he couldn't have asked for a better partner to complement his own skills, sometimes Prussia seemed to harbor a death wish. Most seasoned PIs developed a sixth sense but she brought a whole new magic to the table. "I want you to be careful. Remember the 1926 classic, *The Lodger?* One of our guy's favorite flicks. He goes after a female FBI agent. That should make you think twice about waving yourself around like prime worm. If Schivolsky had the faintest idea . . ."

"He'd wire me up so tight I'd light up the city of Houston," Prussia laughed.

Joe drove silently to the hotel. Over the last several weeks they had cased a number of bars within a narrow radius of the Gutter's drop-off points. Lots of guys had flirted with Prussia, but no one had stepped over the line. Hopefully tonight they'd get lucky.

As they pulled into the hotel parking lot, Prussia said, "Schivolsky secretly likes the idea of using me as bait — only he has to play by the rules. God forbid he endanger a civilian."

Prussia was right. Schivolsky hadn't brought him onto this case for his speed-dial resources or his gut instincts. The police had to play by the rules — and sometimes rules got in the way.

"He wants you to bring him down, Joe. For good."

Joe hated Prussia reading his mind — but when the lady was right, she was right.

Two Weeks Later
The Barnacle, Humble, Texas, 11:00 P.M.

Prussia nodded and smiled at the patrons setting her up. She downed a third shot of apricot brandy, savoring the hot rush pouring through her veins like liquid fire. Coincidence be damned, she didn't expect to connect with the Gutter in a two-bit redneck dive like this. They'd been staking out the bar for more than two weeks without a nibble. Prussia could feel him out there, waiting — *out there* being the operative phrase.

Despite the age difference, Prussia's resemblance to the victims had been sheer luck. The Department couldn't risk a rookie or civilian on a sting like this and their seasoned female officers were too old to attract the Gutter's attention. Schivolsky needed a hardened professional team, and thanks to the Wilsons, he had one.

Out of the corner of her eye, Prussia saw Joe wink as he fanned the deck of cards. A cigar butt hung from his generous lips. Joe knew how to leave a girl alone and let her do her job. "Set me up again, Stan," Prussia said, covertly looking the tall, lean, bartender up and down. Stan's smile testified that there was nothing wrong with his hormones.

For weeks Prussia had opted to stay sober and where had it gotten them? If the Gutter kept to his lunar timetable, they had less than two weeks to score. She suspected vulnerable and available was more his type. The smell of whiskey and tobacco assaulted Prussia as strong, talented hands kneaded her shoulders. One of those hands brushed her hair aside to allow a grizzly beard to tickle her throat. A wave of delicious shivers raced up her spine.

"I'll get that, Stan," the guy chuckled, paying for her drink.

The bartender looked to Prussia. She accepted.

"Dance with me," the owner of those marvelous hands urged. Even whispered, they held the magic of command. The bar's atmosphere quickly changed, becoming smoky, hazy, and warmer than before. The men buying her drinks had been waiting for the booze to turn her will to honey. Little did they suspect she could drink any one of them under the table. Prussia twirled around on the barstool to look Lover Boy over.

Not half bad; tall, and broad-shouldered with heavily lashed blue eyes. A nice mouth. However the country and western travesty on the jukebox made her want to down a bottle of aspirin. "I can't dance to that crap," she said, smiling. He led her to the farthest booth and they talked. His name was Bill Mullen and he owned a nearby ranch. Prussia took his hand. "Prussia Ice," said, relieved to be able to use her real name without breaking protocol. Not being local had its perks. When something decent came on the jukebox, they danced.

Prussia scanned the room from the new angle. No wonder the motley crew at the bar looked so upset. The Barnacle didn't attract the ladies. The music evaporated as a thick, roughened hand worked its way into the armhole of Prussia's shirt. For some reason the guy's nerve made him seem deliciously brave. A lock of hair fell over Bill's forehead, accentuating his puppy dog eyes. He looked like an irresistible but grizzled little boy.

"Wanna go somewhere?" He asked.

Prussia laughed, wondering if he had any idea that for the past seven months a maniac had been wining and dining good-looking girls — then ripping out their guts. "Where you going to take me?" She flirted, sizzling from the feeling of his body against her.

"Heaven," he whispered as the dance ended. Pure, unadulterated common sense won out. Under the circumstances, a one-on-one with a stranger was ill-advised. She glanced at Joe. He seemed more interested in his card game than defending her honor. She was on duty until two when the bar closed and it wasn't even midnight.

"Prussia Ice, huh," Bill laughed, pulling her tightly against him. "You don't feel much like ice to me. Bet no one's ever called *you* an Ice Princess."

Actually, they had. Oh, not in bed, but afterwards, when she walked out, as she invariably did. Bill ordered a gin and tonic for himself. Gut instincts or no, she was pleased he hadn't ordered champagne.

"Come outside," he begged. "I'll protect you."

Prussia giggled. "And who's going to protect me from you?"

Light finally dawned. "Everyone knows me here."

"I don't, and a girl can't be too careful these days."

Bill sighed, like a balloon releasing every last bit of its air. "Guess I can't blame you from being gun-shy, what with all the trouble we've been having around these parts."

Things cooled considerably after her rain of paranoia. Eggs sunny side up, a jolt of orange juice, and some nice clean sheets began to compete with the appeal of sex.

Suddenly, three young girls walked in. Although difficult to tell in the dim light, the one blonde among them didn't appear the Gutter's type. A potential match would have been welcome. Most of Prussia's recent admirers switched their attentions to the three unattached girls, but Bill only had eyes for her. He led her back to the dance floor. Prussia remained watchful as they moved slowly to the music.

Joe was scanning the room, analyzing every lusty stare that passed the blonde's way. He flashed Prussia the coordinates of several men who had remained focused on her despite the much younger competition. Suspect A was too old, late forties. Even from this distance, Prussia could tell he wasn't the type to attract an Alice Wilson or Elizabeth Manfield. Suspect C, a balding man in glasses, wore an off-the rack suit and cheap shoes. Not even worth eye contact.

When the dance ended, Prussia asked Bill to get her a drink, intending to entice Suspect B over. Instead, Stan whispered in her ear. "That blond-haired creep is Beau Slaughter. He's bad news. Give him a wide berth." Stan winked and returned to his spot behind the bar.

Prussia tried to get in touch with her gut. Was she looking at the killer? No bells — no whistles — damn! Mr. Slaughter was attractive in a sleazy kind of way — and he fit the profile. Perhaps Stan might be willing to expound on his warning after close. The three girls had apparently had their fun for the night. They left together and alone, much to the dismay of the nearly all-male crowd. To make matters worse, Bill returned with her drink.

When Bill hit the can, Joe asked her to dance. "Think we struck out?" he asked.

"The bartender warned me about the one guy, Beau Slaughter." Prussia tried, unsuccessfully, to find him in the smoky room.

"He left after the girls. Any chance of you getting away from Lover Boy?" Joe asked. "We could do a drive-by on some of the out-of-the-way spots the Gutter hasn't spoiled yet."

Prussia smiled. "Ah, you want to go parking at some remote lover's lane. What would Kamitria say? If your koochy-mama ever catches you red-handed, she'll make the Gourmet Gutter look like a baby panda."

Joe grinned. "You don't want to get away from him, do you?"

"It's been awhile. I deserve some R&R once I'm off the clock."

"Schivolsky has the parking lot under observation. How's it going to look, you going off with some stranger?" Joe asked.

"Aw, how noble," Prussia teased. "You're afraid someone down at headquarters is going to call me a slut."

"You never know. Your boyfriend could fool us both."

Prussia winked. "Well if you wanta watch, be my guest."

"Does Lover Boy have a name?"

"Bill Mullen." As if summoned, Bill appeared and cut in. Joe smiled, tipped his Stetson, and returned to his game. Bill led Prussia back to her original place at the bar and ordered another round.

Without warning he pulled her towards him. Before she could object, his mouth closed down on hers and his hands slid up the sides of her skirt. Prussia hadn't expected such an ambitious move on his part but crazily, his urgency turned her on.

Other than a few catcalls from the crew to the immediate right, and two or three Peeping Toms moving in for a better view, the only attempted rescue came from Stan the Bartender. "Cool it off guys," he ordered. "Or get a room." Not one to miss an opportunity, Stan sprayed the seltzer bottle directly down her blouse, turning the sheer white cotton virtually invisible. A few shouts and lewd remarks confirmed that she was now, essentially, half-naked.

"Come on, doll, let's go outside," Bill growled.

Prussia stifled a giggle, suddenly realizing why such lines actually worked. It had been weeks since she'd gotten laid. Joe had even started looking good — but there are some excellent reasons not to mess around with your partner. She purred against her will, beyond caring if Bill was the Gourmet Gutter.

An out of uniform Detective Lee walked in. So much for Schivolsky's surveillance. Neither Prussia nor Joe acknowledged him as Lee helped himself to the pot of coffee brewing for close. When he began maneuvering his way towards Prussia, she decided to bolt. Good ol' boys with shifty eyes gave her the chills. The angel on her shoulder warned her to wait for Joe. The devil on the other side hissed: I'm armed. I'm dangerous. I can damn well take care of myself. If Joe wanted to tag along, he was welcome.

Bill led her out to an old white van, the inside of which smelled like fish. "What's that smell?" she asked, wrinkling her nose.

"Crawfish," he replied. "Best eat'n in Texas, present company excepted."

Prussia checked the rearview mirror. It was broken. "Where we going?"

Bill flashed a smile filled with pure good-natured lust. "My place. Unless you don't mind curling up in the back with my critters."

Somehow Prussia couldn't imagine the Gutter digging up crawdaddies. "No thanks."

Ten minutes later they arrived at a small but well-kept ranch house surrounded by pasture. "If you're into horses, we can go out to the stable later," Bill offered, unlocking the door and showing her through a modest living area to the bedroom. "Let me throw this in the dryer for you," he said, relieving her of her wet blouse.

Prussia felt safer once he undressed, as if a serial killer with his pants around his ankles was somehow less threatening. She'd won her share of high school trophies for track and a weekly Tae Kwon Do class kept her in shape. It was hard to believe it had been nine weeks since she had kicked butt.

"Sorry about earlier," Bill rambled. "I had a bit too much to drink. When I saw you . . ."

Prussia finished stripping and lay on the bed.

"God you're beautiful," he finished.

He didn't even turn the lights off. *Good.* She wanted to see him. She wanted to be seen.

Joe pulled the Cavalier off the driveway. The moon illuminated the house and fenced-in pasture beyond. He wiped the sweat from his forehead. *Definitely not New York. It didn't even get livable around here at night.* He resisted the urge to start digging up the place looking for bodies mostly because he already knew he wouldn't find any. Mullen checked out. Schivolsky reported he had a thing for the ladies, but didn't chase chicken. Joe had almost managed to talk himself into going back to the air-conditioned hotel. Almost. After he investigated the van.

Damn. Crawfish! Digging up crawdaddies — one way to find out-of-the-way places to dump bodies. He walked around to the back of the house and located the bedroom window. The shade was only partially down. Sure enough, there was Prussia, naked as a jaybird, banging the guy like there was no tomorrow.

It had been a long day. Only flashes of Prussia's naked body mixed with Jacquelyn's remains kept Joe awake and vigilant. He swatted away a parade of mosquitoes and cussed. Then — an explosion of stars accompanied by excruciating pain sent him spiraling into darkness.

The shadow of a predator undulated jaggedly against the ranch house as he dragged Joe out of sight. Patting him down, he pocketed the .38 Smith & Wesson and checked Joe's I.D. Beau startled as a lone headlight glared in his direction.

Prussia woke abruptly, her hand reaching instinctively for her piece. *Damn.* She'd left her Taurus Snub Nose in her purse. Thank God she hadn't worn a thigh holster tonight and blown her cover even though she felt naked without her 9mm Sig Sauer.

Although the lights had been dimmed, Prussia gradually made out the shadow of a man sitting next to her. He put his hand on her arm. "It's okay, precious. You fell asleep. Bad dream, I guess." She hadn't intended to sleep. "Can I fix you something to eat?" Bill asked.

At the mention of food, alarms went off in her skull — an apt accompaniment to her throbbing headache. "How about some Aspirin?"

"Coming right up. I make a mean Bloody Mary if you have a hangover."

"No thanks," she said, following him into the bathroom. Bill pulled a small cardboard cup from a Dixie dispenser, filled it from the tap, and handed her the bottle of Bayer. Prussia wrinkled up her nose. She didn't like the taste of Houston water.

"Sure you aren't hungry?" he asked again, heading into the kitchen. "I make a mean omelet."

"Eggs sound good." Icy rivers ran uphill along Prussia's spine as she watched him cook, his nakedness only partially obscured by a small apron.

Bill followed her glance. "Don't need to grease up 'Ol' Lightning,'" he jested. "We may need him later on."

"You're incredible." Prussia said.

"Thanks, I try." Bill turned and looked directly into her eyes. "Incredible enough to tempt you to make this here a regular thing?"

"I'm only here short term . . . on business," Prussia said, forcing herself to relax.

"Where you from?"

"Jersey."

"I figured you for a Yank." Bill talked while he cooked. "My dad died a year after I came back from Desert Storm. Left me the farm. My mom went to Louisiana to live with my sister and her family."

Prussia noticed the blue and white cow cookie jar and hand-stenciled recipe. Bill read her mind. "Wife took off about six years ago. Haven't seen or heard from her since."

He served the steaming eggs sunny-side up along with a hot mug of coffee. Prussia waited for him to join her. "Go on and eat," he ordered, slicing up some fresh peaches. "Had a good crop up in Hill Country. Want some sugar with these?"

Prussia took him up on the offer. She was used to sweet Jersey peaches.

"Now, what about you?" Bill asked.

"I travel a lot. I like good food, good wine, walks along the beach —"

Bill roared. "You're not only drop dead gorgeous — you've got one helluva sense of humor to boot." He walked behind her to massage her neck. This time, Prussia cringed. "What's wrong?" he asked.

"I heard something outside." She had.

Bill turned towards the patio doors and switched on the back light. "Probably the horses. Want to walk out to the stable? It's warm enough. No neighbors — you can go as you please."

"No thanks. I'm a city girl. Too many mosquitoes out tonight. If you need to check on them, go on ahead. I'll stay here."

"Suit yourself," he said amiably, pulling on boots left at the back door and exchanging the apron for a robe. "I'll be right back." Prussia hoped Joe had checked Bill out and returned to the hotel. Him playing detective out in the barn would suck — big time.

Since it looked like she'd be spending the night, Prussia found a hiding place for her piece within easy reach, then removed her makeup. To be on the safe side, she checked the place out — not even a lobster in Bill's freezer. Other than a case of hunting rifles and a stack of *Playboys*, the guy was clean.

The cuckoo clock chimed three. Bill had been gone a good twenty minutes. How long could it take to stack hay? She glanced outside as she cleaned up the table. The back light had been switched off, leaving the barn and stables dark. Opening the back door, she called, "Bill?"

There was no answer.

Twenty Minutes Earlier

The killer stood at the end of the driveway, his Harley camouflaged in the nearby brush. Several lights blazed inside the ranch house. He briefly checked out the two empty cars. A flickering beam heading towards the barn caught his attention. Probably the nosy PI, but if he got lucky — it might be Beau, sniffing around after Ice.

Some damn fool was crooning out *Home on the Range*

and pitching hay. Moving closer, the killer identified the figure as Mullen. *Guy must be daft — playing around with horses with a vixen like Ice in his bed! Too bad, Detective Ice — your crazy boyfriend won't be coming back.*

Prussia looked out the front window and squinted into the darkness. Another car was parked next to the Cavalier. She tried Joe's phone. It was turned off. She dialed Schivolsky. He hadn't heard anything from Joe since earlier in the evening when he'd run the check on Mullen. He told her to sit tight. He'd have the constable dispatch backup. *Like hell. Both her partner and some poor schmuck she'd just slept with were out there.*

Prussia slipped out the front door and checked the Cavalier. Locked. No signs of struggle. She glanced longingly at Joe's jacket rolled up in the backseat. Fortunately, she had a key. The custom shotgun would prove difficult to explain to Bill, but she'd deal with that if the time came. Better to go in prepared. She might need more firepower than the Snub Nose.

Something metallic gleamed in the moonlight. Prussia pushed the bushes aside. A Harley, exactly like the one she'd noticed parked back at The Barnacle. Fishing a flashlight out of Joe's emergency cache in the trunk, she headed for the barn.

Beau Slaughter watched from the shadows as the woman knelt over Mullen's body. She put the shotgun down while she checked his vitals. Slaughter made his move. Prussia went down but squirmed out of her assailant's grasp and responded with a fist to his jaw. The hit barely fazed Slaughter but she followed through with an unexpected blow to the knee. He doubled over and howled in pain as Prussia ran for the stable door.

She stumbled, nearly fell. Slaughter caught up with her and ripped off her shirt. Prussia screamed as he hit her again and again, but she refused to go down. Instead, she slipped out of his hold and made a second dash for freedom.

A bike engine roared and throbbed beneath leather-gloved hands. The single beam from a headlight caught Prussia in its surreal glow. She whirled, her eyes huge and wide, like a deer caught in headlights, seemingly more afraid of whatever lurked in the darkness. For a moment she stood frozen, searching the shadows behind her. Framed and backlit, her slim, near-naked form wavered in the illumination.

Focusing on Ice's jutting breasts, Lee licked his lips. "Delectable, Detective," he whispered to himself. An insane laugh erupted like a growl from deep within his throat. "Ah cannot wait to taste those gleam'n cherries."

The cycle roared and charged. At the last second, Ice leapt to safety, rolled and tucked, then slid behind a bale of hay. She went for her gun, but dropped it as a streak of lightning whizzed past her face. Then — everything went to hell in a hand basket. Ice slipped on the slick grass and lost balance. Her head smacked against a rock.

She lay still. Not the way things were supposed to go down. Like a wounded wolf, the Gutter let out a howl of rage that split the night as Beau Slaughter slipped away into the darkness.

Lee found him hiding inside one of the stalls. Standing spread-legged over Mullen's body, Lee herded him out of the shadows with a wave of his gun. There would be questions if the cops found him here, but nothing he couldn't handle — even turn to his advantage. All he had to do was kill Slaughter, then frame him for the last four murders.

"Who are you?" Slaughter demanded, inching forward.

Lee sneered. "Ah bet Bill here would say she's worth dying for," he said, savagely kicking Mullen. "Want to die for her, Beau?"

"Preston Lee?" Slaughter stuttered, going for Henderson's .38. "What the hell!"

Lots of hours at the range had turned Lee into a crack shot. Slaughter's shot went wide as he fell. Didn't matter. A few powder burns to prove self-defense would do nicely. Lee fit a spare revolver into Mullen's hands and fired once at Slaughter. Then, switching sides, he carefully discharged the .38 into Mullen.

He briefly wondered if Henderson was still out cold. It wouldn't do for him to walk in just yet. He had enough to do, arranging the bodies to make it look like a struggle. He didn't want him sniffing around when he went after Ice but with any luck, the big black Dick had seen Slaughter and that would corroborate his story. Regardless, saving Prussia's pretty ass would put Henderson in his debt. Mullen moaned. *Damn! Bastard was still alive!*

Lee heard sirens as he pointed his gun at Mullen a second time. Flashing lights from an overhead pulled into the driveway, temporarily blinding him. He was out of time.

St. Luke's Hospital

Joe refused to be admitted despite a concussion. Bill hadn't been as lucky. Along with the head injury and a cracked rib, he'd taken a bullet in the gut. The surgery had gone well, but Bill was out for the count. Prussia spent the night by his bedside. He woke an hour after dawn.

"You must like it here," Bill said, motioning to the wall clock as Prussia fluffed his pillows.

"Well, you promised me seconds," she teased. "Ol' Lightning up to a rematch?"

Bill laughed. "Shit," he coughed. "That hurts. You better go home and get some sleep or I'll end up busting these stitches."

Prussia filled Bill in on the night's events as hospital personnel led an ongoing parade through his room. Bill bellyached and swore he was ready to go home. Occasionally, he made lewd passes at the nurses. When he finally drifted off to sleep, Prussia walked down the hall to get some coffee. Instead she found Lee. "Hey, aren't you the guy in the big black helmet?"

Lee smiled. "That's me, Easy Rider. Star gazing, huh? No more of them damned apricot brandies for y'all."

"Just like in the cartoons," Prussia parried, "but I try to remember people who save my life. By the way, thank you." Prussia winced. Another Migraine episode. A strobe light flashed. Incomplete images pinched her brain.

"Best find a doctor, Detective. Might have gotten yourself a concussion."

"I'm fine. It's just a Migraine. How did you know Slaughter followed me?"

"Had my eyes on Beau for some time. Son-of-a-bitch had two priors for sexual assault. Officer Woofer and I were still out in the parking lot when he tore out after you and Mullen."

Woofer? Prussia pulled away and walked to the window. A bruised slash of storm clouds hung threateningly over downtown Houston, darkening the emerging sun into a gaping crimson wound. She wrapped her arms around herself.

"Y'all cold?" Lee asked, offering his jacket.

Prussia refused.

"I sure am glad you're okay." Lee squeezed Prussia's hand affectionately. "Perhaps you'd like to have supper with me sometime. I'm a damn fine cook."

Prussia accepted out of sheer politeness.

Eight Days Later

Prussia blew her nose and wiped a cool washcloth over her face. She was still reeling with shock — even after the funeral. The hospital had released Bill the previous week. A neighbor had found him strung up in the barn yesterday. Oddly, even though Humble wasn't in Lee's jurisdiction, thanks to his friendship with Schivolsky, his had been the first car at the scene.

The evidence linking Bill to Beau Slaughter felt really, really wrong. The only proof the two men even knew each other was the note Lee had discovered, conveniently containing a full confession of their involvement in the crimes.

Prussia's cell phone rang. "The results on Wellington are in," Joe said.

"About time. How many times can Records misplace a file? So, anything unusual show up?" Prussia asked.

"Toxicology confirmed a high blood alcohol level and her being drugged. Barbiturate family. Probably why we didn't find any signs of a struggle. I wish we had a better standard of comparison. I'd like to know if the other victims were drugged." Joe paused. "Oh, and like the others, Jacquelyn was raped."

"No surprise there. We already knew the Gutter liked pussy." Prussia said.

Joe set aside his gorilla persona for the milder side he reserved for friends. "Are you okay?"

"Never better," she lied. "Just angry. Joe, Bill was not gay! And he wasn't suicidal."

"I'll take your word for it. For what it's worth, Martha Wilson agrees with you. She dated both Beau and Bill in college. Although Beau turned into a bad seed, apparently, Bill was one of those pillars of the community you always hear about."

"He was framed!" Prussia sobbed. "Lee said they found identical maps of the drop-off points in both Slaughter's gym locker and a filing cabinet in Bill's study but the first team's sweep didn't find any evidence a gym locker existed."

"No shit, Sherlock. The lack of fingerprints tipped me off. People don't wear gloves while handling their own personal effects — and I know one pretty pissed cop who insists the only thing in Mullen's filing cabinet was legal papers. Your boyfriend's not happy about that — or the Wilsons keeping us on retainer another month."

Prussia grit her teeth. "Lee is *not* my boyfriend." During the investigation she had tried to remain neutral about Preston, but Bill's "suicide" had changed things. She'd discovered Lee was the officer involved in the high speed car chase with Somers. Chances were, he'd systematically framed Bill and Beau the same way.

"Good, because if Lee's the Gourmet Gutter — we'll prove it."

"He invited me to dinner next Wednesday. I checked the calendar. It's a full moon."

"Prussia, no," Joe begged. "We're not talking about planting evidence to make a collar. I know you want to clear Mullen's name. We will. All the pieces are falling together. We're in a position of strength now. Just give me some time."

"He screwed up big time trying to frame Bill. It's personal now, Joe. I'll give you a week. You know that's all we have — one week before he kills again."

Night of the Full Moon

While Prussia slipped into a small black dress for her obligatory dinner with Lee, Joe met with Martha Wilson. As they talked, Martha cleaned the glass on her husband's gun cabinet. He had quite a collection. Antiques in the den — a private collection of avant-garde weaponry upstairs. "How far back do you and Preston Lee go?" Joe asked.

Martha stopped polishing and glared at him.

"The Detective in charge of your daughter's case? I thought he was a friend of the family's."

Martha's face reddened. "Why, Detective, where evah did you get that idea? Ah assure you, Preston Lee is certainly no friend of this family."

Joe leaned towards her. "Martha, tell me everything you know about Lee."

He didn't have to ask her twice.

Prussia had just picked up the keys to the Cavalier when her cell phone rang. Probably Joe trying to talk her out of meeting Lee at The Seaside. She'd given him his week. Now it was her turn.

"Thank God I caught you," Joe said. "I finally found something we can use. Lee staged that little rescue out at the Mullen ranch to set us up and make him look like a hero. He lied about being a friend of the Wilsons, too. Martha's terrified of him. They didn't know he was even connected to the case." Joe paused. "I'm still connecting the dots — but what I have makes sense — Lee framing Martha's ex-bed partners — his absolute obsession with food — his infatuation with you." Joe made his final plea. "Trust me on this, Ice. Cancel —"

"I can't. He'll be at the restaurant by now. Plus, he's scheduled to kill again tonight."

"The Seaside Inn," Joe recalled. "I'll take a cab and meet you outside."

"No way," Prussia objected, distracted by the beginning throbs of a killer Migraine. She was dimly aware of Joe talking to Martha Wilson as she searched for her pills.

The Migraine hit. Prussia fell to her knees. Bodies flashed before her eyes — nudes veined in crimson — black and white reminders of the Gutter's handiwork from the department's pin-board. Remnants of nightmares. Darkness.

Twenty minutes later, she came to and quickly donned the shoulder harness for the 9mm. The Browning slid into her thigh holster like a silk glove. She doubted she would need them. By the sound of Joe's voice, he already had an agenda. Schivolsky's pretty boy was going down. Way, way down.

Joe fidgeted in the back of the cab, willing it to fly. "Sorry mister," the cabbie said. "Weekend traffic in the dinner district is always a bitch."

At first Martha had been reluctant to share the specifics about her relationship with Lee but eager to expound on his obsession with food. He'd been into cooking — but it hadn't stopped there. His food fetish carried over into the bedroom. Martha had refused to participate — had, indeed broken things off. She'd confided some disturbing details regarding their last dinner together: Music. Candlelight. Champagne. Truffles and pheasant under glass. A hefty-priced date for a college sophomore. It was then that Joe had made the final connection.

He would never forget the look in Martha's eyes. Comprehension. Revulsion as each grisly detail of her daughter's slaughter flashed through her mind. A true southern lady, Martha's voice remained even and sweet — almost detached. "All the pieces were there." A minute passed. She looked out the window, a perfect portrait of elegance. "Mah sweet little Alice . . . butchered . . . all because of me." Joe wanted to stay and comfort her, but Prussia needed him. As the door closed he heard Martha sob, "Damn him! That bastard tore her heart out!"

Joe was jolted back to the present time and place as a brand-spanking-new bronze Lincoln slammed into the taxi. The ten mile an hour impact wasn't much — just enough to enrage the cabbie and send him yelling and gesticulating into the street. The driver, an immaculately dressed chauffeur, calmly redirected traffic around the accident. He didn't seem to be in a hurry.

Shit — if the car didn't look familiar. Nah, Martha's Lincoln was a moon-dust silver.

Lee swirled the blood-red wine in the crystal glass, watching the tears cascade slowly to the wine's surface. An excellent vintage, although he usually preferred champagne. He had the perfect bottle of Crystal Rose reserved for later. He closed his eyes and smiled as he breathed in the tannic aroma of the bouquet. Cherry. Blackberry. Cinnamon.

Who could have imagined Beau and Bill, same time and place, and after the same woman? Just like old times. Framing them as homo serial killers had been a stroke of genius. Poor, dim, Schivolsky — a pinch of planted evidence and a month without a moon murder should be enough for him to close the case. Surely then, the Wilsons would back off and take Henderson off the payroll.

Lee was so looking forward to this evening. Lovely name, Prussia Ice. Armed, dangerous, and a woman of exquisite taste. He had plans for those cold, cruel eyes of hers. She was a slut just like Molly — a big tease with a black heart and a nasty mouth. It was unfortunate that he could not take her heart.

Detective Lee savored the menu, thinking all the while of a very different cuisine. In a small notepad, he sketched out the display case for the Ice Princess. It had to be fitting. It had to be extravagantly beautiful. And it had to be cold.

It grieved him to forfeit the pleasure of sharing her last moments with the world. Alas, photographs and video of the elaborate exhibit he had so painstakingly designed would have to suffice. As for the corpse, there would be a tragic accident. He couldn't risk anyone connecting Prussia's unfortunate demise to the case.

The waiter cleared his throat. "Excuse me sir. There's a lady waiting for you in reception."

"If she's blonde and good-looking, let her in," Lee said.

"She seems quite adamant you meet her on the terrace."

Lee tipped the waiter and hurried outside into a night filled with electricity. The air smelled of impending rain and the wind promised a record storm. The woman stood silhouetted against a foul, turbulent sky. The light mist obscuring his vision made her seem indistinct like a candle, wavering in the wind. Had the moon loomed huge and full as expected, history might have repeated itself with new consequence. Destiny had been cruel back then. Why had he fallen in love with such a treacherous woman? Looking at her now, he understood. Her long blonde hair floated behind her in the wind. She wore a simple, elegant black dress. Lee kicked himself for falling into the dream again. This wasn't Molly — but Prussia Ice — another cold, heartless whore.

"Prussia?" he said, walking toward her.

The woman turned.

Lee gasped.

Something fizzed through the air with a muffled crack, propelling him backwards. Pain ripped through his gut and he lost his balance, collapsing upon the stone terrace. "Please, Molly, no," he begged, looking up into the barrel of the silencer.

"Y'all didn't think ah'd letcha get away with killing my Alice, did yah?"

The shadow of a large man loomed over Lee. "Mullen? It can't be — you're dead!" Before Lee could scream, a second explosion caught him in the chest. Blood seeped through the Gourmet Gutter's fingers as he clutched the black satin lapels of his jacket.

"Monster," Martha hissed, backing away from the body. "For our baby and all the other girls yah butchered. For Mark, and Beau, God bless their souls. And for mah sweet Bill."

Warren put his hands on his wife's shoulders. "Come on, Molly. Henderson and Ice will be here any minute."

The wind picked up, heralding a record storm as Warren hoisted Lee's body over the terrace wall. The corpse fell into the tangle of thorn bushes in the garden below, a wrought iron post impaling the Gutter like an arrow through his still, icy heart.

A yellow cab sped into the gravel turn. Joe's eyes searched the mist at the back of the terraced restaurant. He could swear he'd seen a woman's figure highlighted against the darkening sky.

Martha stepped back into the shadows. Somewhere, a short distance away, a car door shut and a ghostlike limo slipped into the mist like a silver shadow.

Throwing a wad of bills at the driver, Joe ran like a quarterback possessed, his size twelves sinking into the soft wet turf. By the time he reached the terrace, the woman was gone.

A red Cavalier swung into the parking lot. Headlights brazed the body, tripping over its black wetness like moonlight on dark water.

"Joe!" Prussia called, running towards him.

Joe turned. The Cavalier was still running. Its door was open. Prussia's eyes glowed in the darkness like fire opals — probably just a trick of the moonlight enhanced by too little sleep, but a welcome sight. "Thank you God," he murmured.

The storm clouds parted, releasing a deluge of rain. Henderson and Ice remained to do their job. Moments before a parade of red flashing lights and the song of sirens joined them, the clouds parted to reveal a huge buttery moon. It seemed to smile down upon the rain-soaked corpse, shimmering like an incorporeal halo with the life force of eight fair angels and one southern gentleman.

Contributors

Tom Sweeney is the editor of *Reflections in a Private Eye*, the newsletter of the Private Eye Writers of America. His short stories have been nominated for the Pushcart Prize and the Shamus Award, and have appeared in such diverse publications as *Analog, Blue Murder, Fedora: Private Eyes and Tough Guys,* and *Woman's World*. A native of Massachusetts, he lives with his wife in Portsmouth, New Hampshire.

Dan Sontup sold his first mystery story back in the 1950s. Since then, his stories have appeared in *Alfred Hitchcock's Mystery Magazine, Blue Murder, Ellery Queen's Mystery Magazine, Hardboiled, Mike Shayne Mystery Magazine, Murderous Intent, Thrilling Detective,* and many old pulps and digests. His most recent book publication is "The Santa Switch," a novella in the Eppie Award-winning anthology *Blood, Threat & Fears.*

Stephen D. Rogers' mysteries have appeared or are

forthcoming in *About.com Mysteries, Alternate Realities, Bullet Points, Crimestalker Casebook, Detective Mystery Stories, Ellery Queen's Mystery Magazine, Futures Mysterious Anthology Magazine, HandHeldCrime, Judas, Malone's White Fedora, The Murder Hole, Murderous Intent, The Mystery Review, Mystery Time, MysteryNet, Orchard Press Mysteries, Plots with Guns, Rex Stout Journal,* and *Thrilling Detective.* He writes the mystery column at Writing-World.com and is the mystery department head at *EWG Presents: Without a Clue.* He lives with his family just this side of Cape Cod.

Jack Bludis has been selling books and stories under pseudonyms for almost thirty years, but only recently began using his own name as a byline. He is the author of *The Big Switch* and *The Deal Killer,* both private-eye novels set in Hollywood of the early 1950s. His story, "New Guy on the Block," is set in post-World War II Baltimore and it appears in the anthology, *Mystery Street.* He has lived in and near Baltimore, Maryland, most of his life, but is a frequent visitor to New York City.

Art Montague's short fiction has appeared in *Detective Mystery Stories, HandHeldCrime, Judas, Mysterical-E, Nefarious,* and *Plots with Guns.* Arthur also writes feature articles for *Law and Order Magazine,* reporting on cutting-edge police investigative techniques and administrative processes. A native of Toronto, he has lived in British Columbia and Saskatchewan, and currently resides with his family in Ottawa, Ontario.

More than a dozen of **Carol Kilgore**'s short stories have appeared in *Blue Murder, Bullet Points, TheCase.com,* and *Futures Mysterious Anthology Magazine.* Her flash mystery, "Just a Man on the Sidewalk," received the Short Mystery Fiction Society's Derringer Award for Best Short-Short Mystery in 1999. Another of her stories, "Kidnapped at Noon," was named Publisher's Choice in the June, 2001, issue of *Futures.* She has completed two mystery novels, both featuring Toni Adams, a homicide investigator for the Houston Police Department. A native Houstonian, Carol has lived in a variety of locations across the U.S. She currently resides with her husband in Ruidoso, New Mexico.

Andrew McAleer is the author of *Appearance of Counsel* and the Afterword to the Edgar Award-winning biography, *Rex Stout: A Majesty's Life.* He was born in Boston, in 1967, and took a Bachelors in Philosophy and English Literature from Boston College and a *Juris* Doctor from MSL at Andover. He has contributed to numerous crime literature journals including *The Baker Street Dispatch, Mystery Scene,* and *Mystery Time.* His essays about law and lawyers include a critical analysis of the Lizzie Borden Grand Jury and the History of Suffolk Law School. President of the Boston Authors Club, McAleer practices law privately in Massachusetts and is an adjunct professor of law at Bay State College in Boston.

Linda Summers Posey is the author of more than 200 articles published in the *Houston Chronicle, Oilways, Shell*

News, Texas Highways, and other publications. Her numerous writing awards include first place for mystery-suspense novel manuscript, Houston Writers Conference, and for mystery short story, Fort Bend Writers' Guild. She also placed in the Karen Besecker Memorial Contest for Mystery Writers and a *Byline Magazine* short story contest; won honorable mention in a *Writer's Digest* "Your Assignment" contest; and received several awards for marketing communications. Linda recently completed her first mystery novel featuring Stacy McReady; a second Stacy short story will soon be published. A native Texan, Linda lives with her husband in Houston.

Dorothy Rellas authored the romantic suspense novel *Hidden Motives,* and has just finished her first PI novel. Her short fiction and articles on writing have appeared in *Futures Mysterious Anthology Magazine,* the Sisters in Crime Los Angeles Chapter anthology *A Deadly Dozen,* and an MWA/UCLA Writers Program handbook. She lives with her family in Pasadena, California.

Kenneth Thornton Samuels is the pseudonym adopted by Midwestern police officer Jim Doherty for what he hopes will be the first of many stories about Windy City private eye Errol Pucinski. Under his own name, Doherty has written an award-winning series of police procedurals, featuring roving cop Dan Sullivan, which have appeared in *Blue Murder, Mystery Buff,* and *Over My Dead Body!* As Scott Morrison, he's started a series of mystery/western hybrids featuring frontier Pinkerton operative Mike Segretto, the first of which was published in

HandHeldCrime. Born in San Francisco, he lives in Chicago with his wife, Katy.

Nick Andreychuk's short crime fiction has appeared in *Crimestalker Casebook, Detective Mystery Stories, Fedora: Private Eyes and Tough Guys, Futures Mysterious Anthology Magazine, Mystery Time, Nefarious, Rex Stout Journal,* and many other publications. The Short Mystery Fiction Society honored his story "In the Heat of the Moment" with a Derringer Award. This story can be found in *Bullet Points,* an anthology of short-short mystery fiction that Andreychuk co-edited. Born in Ontario, Canada, he currently resides in British Columbia, where he operates a coffeehouse with his wife.

Robert Lopresti is the author of more than twenty-five short stories which have appeared in *Alfred Hitchcock's Mystery Magazine, TheCase.com, Mike Shayne Mystery Magazine, Murderous Intent,* and *New Crimes,* among other publications. One of his stories about Atlantic City private eye Marty Crow was a nominee for the Anthony Award for best mystery short story. A New Jersey native, he now lives in Bellingham, Washington.

Tim Wohlforth's short stories have appeared in *Bullet Points, Detective Mystery Stories, EWG Presents: Without a Clue, Fedora: Private Eyes and Tough Guys, HandHeld-Crime, Mysterical-E, Over My Dead Body,* and *Plots with Guns.* He recently co-authored the non-fiction book, *On*

The Edge: Political Cults Right and Left. He moderated the short story panel at Left Coast Crime in Portland and is presently circulating a mystery novel featuring PI Jim Wolf.

D. **Jeanette McSherry**'s short fiction and poetry have appeared in *Flashquake, Pathway to Darkness,* and *Suddenly I, II, III,* and *IV,* and she recently completed her first horror novel. Jeanette has served as the Conference Chair and Competition Chair for the Woodlands Writer's Guild annual Writers Conference. Born in Springfield, Missouri, Jeanette spent most of her life in New Jersey. She currently resides with her family in Spring, Texas.

About the Editor

Michael Bracken is the author of *All White Girls, Bad Girls, Canvas Bleeding, Deadly Campaign, Even Roses Bleed, In the Town of Dreams Unborn and Memories Dying, Just in Time for Love, Psi Cops, Tequila Sunrise,* and nearly 800 shorter works. He previously edited *Fedora: Private Eyes and Tough Guys,* a collection of hard-boiled crime fiction. Bracken has received numerous awards for advertising copywriting and his short story, "Cuts Like a Knife," was nominated for a Derringer Award. Born in Canton, Ohio, Bracken has traveled extensively throughout the U.S., and currently resides with his family in Waco, Texas.

www.ingramcontent.com/pod-product-compliance
Lightning Source LLC
Chambersburg PA
CBHW020613310726
48979CB00008B/1465/J

* 9 7 8 1 5 9 2 2 4 9 4 9 7 *